Orders Is Orders

SELECTED FICTION WORKS BY L. RON HUBBARD

FANTASY

The Case of the Friendly Corpse

Death's Deputy

Fear

The Ghoul

The Indigestible Triton

Slaves of Sleep & The Masters of Sleep

Typewriter in the Sky

The Ultimate Adventure

SCIENCE FICTION

Battlefield Earth

The Conquest of Space

The End Is Not Yet

Final Blackout

The Kilkenny Cats

The Kingslayer

The Mission Earth Dekalogy*

Ole Doc Methuselah

To the Stars

ADVENTURE

The Hell Job series

WESTERN

Buckskin Brigades

Empty Saddles

Guns of Mark Jardine

Hot Lead Payoff

A full list of L. Ron Hubbard's
novellas and short stories is provided at the back.

*Dekalogy—a group of ten volumes

L. RON HUBBARD

Orders Is Orders

GALAXY PRESS

Published by
Galaxy Press, LLC
7051 Hollywood Boulevard, Suite 200
Hollywood, CA 90028

Printed in the United States of America.

ISBN-10 1-59212-295-7
ISBN-13 978-1-59212-295-0

Library of Congress Control Number: 2007928446

Contents

Stories from Pulp Fiction's Golden Age

A ND it *was* a golden age.
The 1930s and 1940s were a vibrant, seminal time for a gigantic audience of eager readers, probably the largest per capita audience of readers in American history. The magazine racks were chock-full of publications with ragged trims, garish cover art, cheap brown pulp paper, low cover prices—and the most excitement you could hold in your hands.

"Pulp" magazines, named for their rough-cut, pulpwood paper, were a vehicle for more amazing tales than Scheherazade could have told in a million and one nights. Set apart from higher-class "slick" magazines, printed on fancy glossy paper with quality artwork and superior production values, the pulps were for the "rest of us," adventure story after adventure story for people who liked to *read*. Pulp fiction authors were no-holds-barred entertainers—real storytellers. They were more interested in a thrilling plot twist, a horrific villain or a white-knuckle adventure than they were in lavish prose or convoluted metaphors.

The sheer volume of tales released during this wondrous golden age remains unmatched in any other period of literary history—hundreds of thousands of published stories in over nine hundred different magazines. Some titles lasted only an issue or two; many magazines succumbed to paper shortages during World War II, while others endured for decades yet. Pulp fiction remains as a treasure trove of stories you can read, stories you can love, stories you can remember. The stories were driven by plot and character, with grand heroes, terrible villains, beautiful damsels (often in distress), diabolical plots, amazing places, breathless romances. The readers wanted to be taken beyond the mundane, to live adventures far removed from their ordinary lives—and the pulps rarely failed to deliver.

In that regard, pulp fiction stands in the tradition of all memorable literature. For as history has shown, good stories are much more than fancy prose. William Shakespeare, Charles Dickens, Jules Verne, Alexandre Dumas—many of the greatest literary figures wrote their fiction for the readers, not simply literary colleagues and academic admirers. And writers for pulp magazines were no exception. These publications reached an audience that dwarfed the circulations of today's short story magazines. Issues of the pulps were scooped up and read by over thirty million avid readers each month.

Because pulp fiction writers were often paid no more than a cent a word, they had to become prolific or starve. They also had to write aggressively. As Richard Kyle, publisher and editor of *Argosy*, the first and most long-lived of the pulps, so pointedly explained: "The pulp magazine writers, the best of them, worked for markets that did not write for critics or attempt to satisfy timid advertisers. Not having to answer to anyone other than their readers, they wrote about human beings on the edges of the unknown, in those new lands the future would explore. They wrote for what we would become, not for what we had already been."

Some of the more lasting names that graced the pulps include H. P. Lovecraft, Edgar Rice Burroughs, Robert E. Howard, Max Brand, Louis L'Amour, Elmore Leonard, Dashiell Hammett, Raymond Chandler, Erle Stanley Gardner, John D. MacDonald, Ray Bradbury, Isaac Asimov, Robert Heinlein—and, of course, L. Ron Hubbard.

In a word, he was among the most prolific and popular writers of the era. He was also the most enduring—hence this series—and certainly among the most legendary. It all began only months after he first tried his hand at fiction, with L. Ron Hubbard tales appearing in *Thrilling Adventures, Argosy, Five-Novels Monthly, Detective Fiction Weekly, Top-Notch, Texas Ranger, War Birds, Western Stories,* even *Romantic Range.* He could write on any subject, in any genre, from jungle explorers to deep-sea divers, from G-men and gangsters, cowboys and flying aces to mountain climbers, hard-boiled detectives and spies. But he really began to shine when he turned his talent to science fiction and fantasy of which he authored nearly fifty novels or novelettes to forever change the shape of those genres.

Following in the tradition of such famed authors as Herman Melville, Mark Twain, Jack London and Ernest Hemingway, Ron Hubbard actually lived adventures that his own characters would have admired—as an ethnologist among primitive tribes, as prospector and engineer in hostile climes, as a captain of vessels on four oceans. He even wrote a series of articles for *Argosy*, called "Hell Job," in which he lived and told of the most dangerous professions a man could put his hand to.

Finally, and just for good measure, he was also an accomplished photographer, artist, filmmaker, musician and educator. But he was first and foremost a *writer*, and that's the L. Ron Hubbard we come to know through the pages of this volume.

This library of Stories from the Golden Age presents the best of L. Ron Hubbard's fiction from the heyday of storytelling, the Golden Age of the pulp magazines. In these eighty volumes, readers are treated to a full banquet of 153 stories, a kaleidoscope of tales representing every imaginable genre: science fiction, fantasy, western, mystery, thriller, horror, even romance—action of all kinds and in all places.

Because the pulps themselves were printed on such inexpensive paper with high acid content, issues were not meant to endure. As the years go by, the original issues of every pulp from *Argosy* through *Zeppelin Stories* continue crumbling into brittle, brown dust. This library preserves the L. Ron Hubbard tales from that era, presented with a distinctive look that brings back the nostalgic flavor of those times.

L. Ron Hubbard's Stories from the Golden Age has something for every taste, every reader. These tales will return you to a time when fiction was good clean entertainment and the most fun a kid could have on a rainy afternoon or the best thing an adult could enjoy after a long day at work.

Pick up a volume, and remember what reading is supposed to be all about. Remember curling up with a *great story*.

—Kevin J. Anderson

KEVIN J. ANDERSON *is the author of more than ninety critically acclaimed works of speculative fiction, including* The Saga of Seven Suns, *the continuation of the Dune Chronicles with Brian Herbert, and his* New York Times *bestselling novelization of L. Ron Hubbard's* Ai! Pedrito!

Orders Is Orders

Chapter One

THE doomed city of Shunkien poured flame-torn billows of smoke skyward to hide the sun. Mile after square mile spread the smoldering expanse of crumbling walls and corpse-littered streets.

And still from the Peking area came the bombers of the Rising Sun to further wreck the ruins. Compact squadrons scudding through the pall of greasy smoke turned, dived, zoomed, leaving black mushrooms swiftly growing behind their racing shadows.

Along a high bluff to the north of town, a line of artillery emplacements belched flame and thunder, and mustard-colored men ministered to their plunging guns.

Japan was pounding wreckage into ashes, wiping out a city which had thrived since the time of Genghis Khan, obliterating a railhead to prevent further concentration of Chinese legions.

Down amid the erupting shambles, three regiments of Chinese troops held on, bellies to dust behind barricades of paving stones, sandbags and barbed wire, shoulders wedged into the embrasures of the cracking walls, intent brown eyes to antiaircraft sights in the uprooted railway station.

They fought because they could not retreat. Two hundred

miles and two Japanese army corps stood between them and the sea. Somewhere out in the once-fertile plains two Chinese armies groped for the enemy. But the battle lines were everywhere, running parallel to nothing, a huge labyrinth of war engines and marching legions. There was no hope for Shunkien. Once proud signs protruded from the rubble which overlaid the gutters. The thoroughfares were dotted with the unburied dead, men and women and children. Thicker were these ragged bundles near the south gate where lines of refugees had striven to leave the town, only to be blasted down at the very exit.

The cannonading was a deafening monotone. The smoke and dust drifted and entwined. Walls wearily slid outward, slowly at first, then faster to crash with a roar, making an echo to the thunder of artillery along the ridge.

War was here, with Famine on the right and Death upon the left and Pestilence riding rear guard to make the sweep complete.

In the center of the city, close by a boulevard now gutted with shell holes and clogged with wrecked trolleys and automobiles and inert bodies, stood the United States Consulate.

The gates were tightly closed and the walls were still intact and high above, on a tall flagstaff, buffeted by the concussion of shells, Old Glory stood brightly out against the darkness of the smoke.

The building was small and the corridors were jammed with the hundred and sixteen Americans who had taken refuge there. Without baggage, glad enough to be still alive, they sat in groups and nursed their cigarettes and grinned and cracked jokes and made bets on their chances of being missed by all the shells which came shrieking down into the town.

It was hard to talk above the ceaseless roar, but they talked. Talked of Hoboken and Sioux City and Denver and argued the superior merits of their towns. Though their all was invested in and about Shunkien, though most of them had not been home for years, Frisco and Chi and the Big Town furnished the whole of their conversation.

A baby was crying and its white-faced mother tried to sing above the cataract of sound which beat against the walls outside. A machinery salesman tore his linen handkerchief into small bits and stuffed fragments of it into the child's ears. Thankfully, it stopped whimpering and the mother smiled and the salesman, suddenly finding himself caught, moved hurriedly away before he could be thanked.

Within the consular office, the consul, Thomas Jackson, moved to the side of his radio operator. Jackson was white-haired, small, nervous of face and hands. He looked at the expanse of gleaming dials as though trying to read hope in their metal faces.

The operator, a youth scarcely out of his teens, leaned over a key and rattled it. He threw a switch and pressed the earphones against his head. He lighted a cigarette with nicotine-stained fingers and stuck it in his mouth. He pulled a typewriter to him and began to write.

"I've got Shanghai again, sir," said the operator. "They want to know how we're holding out."

"Tell them we're all right so far, and God knows we've been

lucky." Jackson leaned close to the operator and then glanced around to see that no one else in the room could hear. "Tell them for the love of God to get the cholera antitoxin to us if they expect to find any of us alive after this is over. Tell them Asiatic cholera is certain to follow, has already begun. And then tell them that we've got to have money—gold. Our checks and paper are no good and the food is running low."

The young operator precariously perched his cigarette on the already burned edge of his table and began to make the bug click and quiver.

A few minutes later he beckoned to the consul. "They say the USS *Miami* is already proceeding down the coast with both the serum and the money."

"Damned little good that will do us," moaned Jackson. "A cruiser can't come two hundred miles inland."

"They said they'd try to get it through to us, sir. They want to know how long we can hold out."

Jackson ran bony fingers through his awry white hair and looked around him. He singled out a fat little man whose eyes were so deep in his head they could not be seen at all.

"Doctor," said Jackson, loud enough to be heard above the cannonade but not loud enough for anyone else to overhear, "Doctor, how long do you think we can last without the cholera shots?"

"With corpses strewn from Hell to Halifax?" puffed the doctor. "Now, tomorrow, next week, maybe never."

"Please," begged the consul, "you're not staking your reputation on this. How long will it take?"

"The reports are," said the doctor, "that it is just now

starting to spread. I'll give it five days to reach here because, in five days, we'll have to start going out to buy food—if we can find the gold with which to buy it. Otherwise, we stay here bottled up, boil our water and starve to death. We all had cholera shots before we came into this area, but they won't prove effective unless bolstered with secondary, epidemic shots. If we get that serum here before Saturday, there's a chance of our living—as far as disease is concerned—through this mess. But mind you, now, you can't quote me. Anything is liable to happen."

"Thanks," said Jackson gratefully.

The consul went back to the youth at the key. "Tell them it's got to be here by Saturday, Billy. Not a day later. Though how they'll get it here, only God himself can tell."

He looked out through the office door into the outside passageway where a hundred and more Americans tried to take it calmly. The floor of the consulate was shaking as though a procession of huge trucks rumbled deafeningly by.

Chapter Two

THE USS *Miami*, taperingly sleek and gray, with black smoke still pouring from her funnels, dropped anchor thunderously in the yellow roadstead off Liaochow and swung around in the stream of the tide.

From the bridge the coastal city of Liaochow presented a dismal sight. Two air raids and an offshore shelling by the Japanese men-o'-war had rid the place of Chinese defense and the flames still smoldered amid the festering ruins.

A dark horde of Japanese destroyers and cruisers and troopships lay at anchor near the shore and launches were carrying load after load of Japanese troops to the landings. Lighters behind struggling tugs were deep with howitzers and tanks bound for various destinations along a two-thousand-mile front which stretched from Peking to Shanghai.

His cruiser riding aloof and alone, the Navy captain surveyed the cluttered, smoky waterfront through his glasses. Then, hopelessly, he let the binoculars thump against his chest and thrust his big red hands into the pockets of his coat, scowling at the panorama of devastation.

"We haven't got a chance," he said.

The younger officer beside him, his exec, not bearing all the responsibility, was less downcast. "Oh, I'm certain we can find some way, sir. After all, *we're* not at war with Japan or China. As a strictly neutral . . ."

"Yes. Sure. Strictly neutral!" growled the captain. "I've got my orders, sir. I've got my orders from the C-in-C himself. I am to avoid any slightest possibility of allowing Japan to create an 'incident.'" He said this bitterly as though a few hearty salvos would have done him a world of good.

Behind him respectfully stood two lieutenants, pilots of the scout planes, and a hard-faced captain of Marines.

"I think," said one of the pilots, "that if you let Richards and me take off, we could make it through—"

"You *think*!" barked the captain acidly. "You're not supposed to *think*! Do you suppose for one minute that I'd be fool enough to let you and Lieutenant Richards go blasting halfway across China armed and aching for a scrap?"

"But sir," said Richards, "I think—"

"You think too, do you? Well, see here, both of you. I appreciate the fact that medals and glory and publicity might be attractive, but the responsibility is mine and as long as it *is* mine, I'll decide this affair. Shunkien is two hundred miles inland. The rails are blown up. At least four armies are fighting between here and there. And what would happen if I let two battle planes go skipping over that area? There'd be a protest at the very least and a severe reprimand for me. And quite probably some enthusiastic such-and-so would dive on you and you'd fix his clock and then the United States would be in it up to our necks."

The captain of Marines, whose face was as tough and hard as walnut and whose left breast was laddered with campaign ribbons, coughed for recognition. "Sir, if you'd let me take my company—"

"So you're thinking too, are you?" sizzled the badgered captain. "You're itching to get that company of yours over there. And what would happen then? A sniper would let you have it. A machine gunner would accidentally rake you. And the first thing you know, one company of Marines would be trying to mop up half a million yellow troops. No, thank you, Captain Davis. I know my Marines. There are at least four armies and two lines of battle between here and Shunkien. You could never make it without getting into a fight. Whether Japan declared it or not, this is *war!*"

Desolately they stared at the smoking town and the inexhaustible streams of Japanese troops being disgorged from the troopships.

"Sir," said the captain of Marines, "it's certain that the money and serum has to get to Shunkien and if you won't trust your planes or my company, maybe one or two men on foot could make it. If they get killed, the United States won't go to war over two Marines. And they could not create much damage."

"I see you've had this in mind all along," accused the commanding officer.

"Yessir. As soon as I heard what had to be done I remembered that my gunnery sergeant, James Mitchell, was born in this province—in Yin-Meng, I think it was. They had him on intelligence work out of the Peking Legation because he speaks three of the northern dialects."

The captain pursed his lips thoughtfully and scowled at

the deck. He looked up. "Didn't you threaten to bobtail one of your sergeants for being drunk and overleave in Shanghai last week? Wasn't his name Mitchell?"

Caught, the Marine officer made the best of it. "Yessir, that's Mitchell, sir. The captain has a good memory."

"The captain has to have a good memory around you pirates," said the commanding officer gruffly. "What's the rest of his record?"

"Obedience 4.0, everything 4.0. Except sobriety, and that's down to 2.5. But there's no chance of his getting drunk over there, sir. Certainly not on duty."

The commanding officer was thinking again. "If I recall, he came to you a private first class and you gave him his stripes back. Was he bobtailed at Peking?"

"Yessir. You see, he was off duty in the Native Quarter and—"

"Why did you make him again?"

"Well, sir, a man like Mitchell won't stay down. He's very intelligent and sets an excellent example for the men. He's young and makes a good-looking Marine. His father is a missionary."

"*That's* no recommendation," said the captain.

"I know," replied the captain of Marines. "But the kid had good enough sense to pull out from China when he was fifteen. He kicked around the States and then enlisted and he's on his second hitch now. He knows this country and if anybody can get through to Shunkien, it's Mitchell."

"You actually advise me to send a drunk on a mission like this?"

"I don't think he'll do any drinking on duty, sir. He knows his own weakness. If he takes one drink, he can't stop. But he won't run across any whisky ashore with everything cut up like it is."

"Are you certain he has never drunk on duty?"

"Well, only once, sir. Or maybe twice. But if he realizes the gravity of this situation . . ." He let it hang there.

The commanding officer surveyed the shoreline again. His face was screwed into a knot of perplexity. And as he watched, a man came down from the radio shack and thrust a message into his hand.

The captain read it with a set jaw and then balled it into a wad.

"They're pleading with us now," he snapped. "Was there ever an officer who had more trouble than me? Captain Davis, who would you send through with this gunnery sergeant? No officer, mind you. If an officer got killed, there'd be an 'incident.'"

"Spivits, private first class, came aboard with Mitchell, sir. They were on a lot of assignments in North China."

"Who and what is this Spivits, first class?"

"He's a twenty-year man, sir."

"What? And still a private?"

"Yessir. He's one of these professional privates, sir. He's a good man. Onetime heavyweight champ of the Atlantic Fleet. But he doesn't want to be rated, protests against it. He's an expert rifleman and though he might not be exactly an Adonis and though he might have a few blind spots, he's a good man to have along in a scrap."

13

The commanding officer sighed deeply and shoved his big red hands deeper into his coat pockets. He seemed to be supporting an entire fleet on his shoulders.

"Well, there's one consolation. If they're killed, there won't be much of a ripple about it, and if they get through, I've done my duty regardless. Carry on, Captain Davis."

He turned around and studied the shore again and the Marine captain jubilantly trod upon Richards' toe, saluted and hurried away.

Chapter Three

SITTING cross-legged like an Indian on the edge of an OD blanket, Jimmy Mitchell was losing his all at blackjack. His green cap was on the back of his head and the sweat of exertion bedewed his brow. A cigarette, cocked skyward in a futile attempt to keep the smoke out of his eyes, placed a perfect screen across his vision. But the smoke was not thick enough to obscure the fact that the sergeant across the blanket was turning up a queen and an ace.

Mitchell paid off and passed the deal. He clinked two Mex twenty-cent pieces forlornly together, put them out, got thirteen, drew a king on his hit, and therefore, busted in more ways than one, withdrew from the blanket on the hatch.

He stood up stiffly and flexed his arms. He yawned elaborately to show that he didn't care, cocked his cap over his right eye so precariously that it was in danger of falling and walked toward a porthole.

He stared out at the brass-framed view of the dark Japanese men-o'-war and the hurrying launches and the smoldering city and leaned his elbow against a steam pipe to contemplate it.

He was tall even for a Marine, and there was a certain ease about him which comes of constant training, good rations and an alert profession. He showed good breeding in the clean, regular features and his brisk blue eyes sparkled with intelligence. He was the sort of man a company commander instantly selects for rating with a sigh of relief.

Several Marines had been watching the shore from the next port and now, seeing their gunnery sergeant taking an interest in the scenery, they moved down the line and stood about him, peering over his shoulder and around his arm at the beach as though that was the only possible vantage point on the whole ship.

"Boy, wouldn't I like to see something start around here," said a boot with vague, romantic notions about war.

Mitchell turned and surveyed the youth quietly. He looked from the brown bulldog toes of his shoes, up the creases of his green pants, up the length of khaki-colored tie and then, at last, at the speaker's face. Without saying a word, Mitchell turned and looked at the shore again. The boot reddened.

A growling, rumbling voice, so deep that it appeared to come from at least the engine room, said, "You do your wishin' in private, sonny, and leave your betters alone."

The boot spun about to stare up at the battered visage of Toughey Spivits.

Toughey had been hit in the larynx with a steel-shod rifle butt at Château-Thierry and had talked that way ever since. It was a very ominous thing, that voice.

"I just said—" began the boot.

"So you'd like to mix it," rumbled Toughey. "Why, one of those little Japanese would take just one bite and you'd be in two chunks."

"But it gets so monotonous standing off and on and hearing all that scrapping going on," protested the boot.

"It wouldn't be half as monotonous as pushin' up posies till Gabriel yells for you to grab your socks."

"But don't *you* want to get ashore?" persisted the boot.

"Sonny," said Toughey Spivits, "you couldn't get me to set foot on that beach for a million, million bucks, s'help me."

"You mean you're scared?"

"Of course I'm scared. It takes sense to get scared, don't it, Sarge?"

"Yeah," said Mitchell.

"But you been fightin' over here before," said the boot eagerly. "It couldn't be so bad if you came back to do some more."

"I got the habit," said Toughey.

"Aw, nuts," said a corporal. "You're just itchin' to get over there and mop up some of those yellow-bellies and you know it."

"Not me," said Toughey. "I got brains enough to be scared. Why, if I so much as hear a bullet anymore I get pale and shake all over. Once the sarge and me was out gettin' some dope and I thinks I hear a shot and an hour later I come to in the grass with the sarge pourin' water all over me. 'I'm dead,' I says. 'That shot got me right in the heart.' 'What shot?' says the sarge. 'That was just me closin' my cigarette case.'"

The boot gaped up at Toughey's serious face for ten seconds before the stifled laughter around him exploded.

"Aw, go on," said the boot. "You're just shootin' the breeze. Ain't he, Sarge?"

"Gospel truth," said Mitchell, turning. "And I think he's right. It sure would take a case of gin to make me head for that dock. Those Japanese are just aching to shoot people up. And the hell of it is, they're doing it."

"What're we up here for?" said the corporal.

"Well, the admiral told me yesterday," said Mitchell, "that we was out of soda water."

"Aw," said the corporal, "don't nobody know nothin'?"

"All I know is," said Mitchell, "I'm hopin' nobody gets any bright ideas and makes us go ashore. I tell you if they had cases of gin stacked ten feet high from one end of that wharf to the other, and if the skipper told me to go in and take all I could carry in a motor sailer, I still *wouldn't*—"

The brass-voiced loudspeaker on the bulkhead rasped, "James Mitchell, gunnery sergeant, report to Captain Davis at the starboard gangway. James Mitchell, gunnery sergeant, report to Captain Davis at the starboard gangway."

Mitchell hastily set his cap to rights and straightened his khaki tie to make the ends exactly even.

But before he had gone a step, the speaker clicked on again. "A. A. Spivits, private first class, report to Captain Davis at the starboard gangway. A. A. Spivits, private first class, report to Captain Davis at the starboard gangway."

Spivits hastily fixed his own tie and straightened up his great height.

"Looks like the skipper wants our advice," said Toughey to the group and then lumbered after the hurrying Mitchell.

A few seconds later they stood before Captain Davis on the white deck planking with the offshore wind undoing all the tie-straightening.

"Sergeant," said Davis, "there are two items to be delivered to Shunkien." He said it as though Shunkien was about as far from there as the torpedo tubes. "I have suggested that you and Private Spivits might volunteer to take them."

"Yes, sir," said Mitchell, as though Shunkien was no farther from there than the stanchion to his right.

"Yes, sir," said Spivits quickly, as though he was, at that moment, in the very center of Shunkien.

"Good," said the walnut-faced captain. "Report in a half-hour, full pack."

Mitchell and Spivits saluted, about-faced and rattled down the companionway and out of sight.

The exec appeared at Davis' left. "The captain wants to see you again."

They went forward and found the Navy captain still studying the shore with great attention. He did not turn. "You might impress your two men with the fact that they are not to create any disturbances ashore."

"Yes, sir," said Davis.

"And you might also tell them that I have just received word that there are three major offensives in progress between here and Shunkien. They will be forced to pass through those armies." He turned and cleared his throat. "Damn it, Davis, this is a long chance. But it's certain that two Marines can't do much damage and it's equally certain that we won't go to war over the disappearance of two Marines. If it weren't for the repeated requests from Shunkien . . ." He shrugged. "There's the keg."

A sailor lugged it down to the starboard gangway. A hospital corpsman came up with the carefully packed package of serum. He stood by, waiting to give it up.

"I get the drift of this," said the corpsman to the seaman. "Those two leathernecks are outward bound for Shunkien."

"Jesus," said the seaman, startled. "Through all that mess ashore?"

"I wouldn't give a secondhand swab for their chances," said the corpsman.

"Aw, well, hell," replied the sailor. "What's a couple of Marines?"

Below, Mitchell was loading his pistol clips with newly issued ammunition. He was thoughtfully methodical about it, as though he had no other destination than the range in prospect.

Finishing the task, he slid the spares into the pouch on his web belt and hitched his holster into a comfortable position. He took his pack and, standing before his opened locker, began to insert his razor and shaving brush and other toilet articles. As he moved the contents of the shelf about, a bottle at the extreme back caught his eye.

He reached for it and pulled it into the light, speculatively reading the label which said *Canadian Whisky. Five Years Old. One Quart.*

He started to put it back and stopped. Reluctantly, as though he could not stay his hand, he took his extra shoes out of his pack and put the bottle in their place.

Twice he started to take it out again but it required more willpower than he could summon at the moment.

"Might as well carry dynamite," he said ruefully.

He shrugged into his shoulder straps and snapped them into place. He picked up Toughey on his way out and together they mounted to the starboard gangway.

Captain Davis handed his gunnery sergeant a sheaf of orders. "Take care of these. Here's the keg and the box. Take care of them and deliver them, intact, to Consul Jackson, United States Consulate at Shunkien. Understand?"

"Yessir," said Mitchell. "Take the keg, Toughey."

Toughey boosted the keg up to his mighty shoulder and steadied it there. Mitchell tied the box to his web belt.

"Is that all, sir?" said Mitchell.

"Yes. Carry on, Sergeant."

Mitchell and Toughey saluted and started down the gangway toward the nervously putt-putting motor sailer which had been put into the water. The captain touched Mitchell's shoulder, stopping him for an instant.

"I wish you luck, Sergeant."

"Thank you, sir."

"And Sergeant . . . be careful about the booze, will you? It's pretty important that you get to Shunkien."

"Oh, you bet, sir."

Captain Davis took his hand and shook it. "If . . . that is . . . if I don't see you again . . . well . . . here's luck."

Mitchell said, "Thank you, sir," and went on down the ladder into the motor sailer. When he sat down and leaned against the gunwale, a sharp edge of the whisky bottle gouged him through his pack. He moved uncomfortably.

They watched the ship shorten and crouch into the waves.

The smoldering city grew larger as they picked their way through the multitudinous launches and ships.

With a jingle of bells, the motor sailer swerved in toward the float and a sailor bounced out to hold the boat. Mitchell and Toughey got out.

"So long," said the coxswain.

"So long," said Mitchell.

They walked up the ramp to the dock and marched around piled war supplies to reach the bustling street beyond.

Behind them, the USS *Miami* had vanished through a screen of Japanese war vessels and low-lying smoke.

Chapter Four

L IAOCHOW presented a bleak picture to Mitchell and
Spivits, one they had seen many times before in other
longitudes. The last bombardment of the city had taken place
not thirty-six hours before and just now impressed Chinese
and commandeered trucks were beginning to fumble through
the wreckage.

Corpses in various stages of completeness and the fragments
thereof were being tossed helter-skelter into conveyances.
Dismal crews were poking into the rubble of fallen walls,
unearthing chunks of this and that and adding them to the
battered and tattered cargoes.

Troop lorries and moistly burdened trucks alternated on
the westerly road from town and the two sea-soldiers in green
were forced to stop time and again to keep from being run down.

Toughey Spivits manfully bore up under the sixty-pound
keg. The weight of rifle and pack, added to this, drew the
sweat from his broad brow and took his wind.

They were in a suburb of the town when Mitchell called a
halt so that he could choose between two roadways. Toughey
thumped the keg to the ground and sat upon it, swabbing
out his cap band and then selecting a cigarette from it.

"Wonder what's in this thing," said Toughey, scratching a
match on the keg.

"Never mind what's in it," replied Mitchell. "All I know is, it's going to Shunkien and in Shunkien it'll arrive. This is Tuesday, isn't it?"

"Yeah," said Toughey.

"My orders is that we get this to Shunkien on Saturday. We got to average fifty miles a day."

"Fifty miles a day!" growled Toughey. "Hell, Sarge, we can't hoof it that fast. Not with this damned thing draggin' me down like a sea anchor. It just ain't human, that's what."

"Who said anything about anybody bein' human?" replied Mitchell. "If your scuppers are under, I'll take it."

"Hell, it ain't heavy. Do I hear guns?"

"It isn't a symphony orchestra, that's a cinch. They must be fighting out there someplace."

"How we going to get through a battle?"

Mitchell shrugged. "How we going to get through *two* battles? Say, wait a minute. Don't say I never take care of my troops."

Mitchell let out a string of Chinese and walked across the street. Toughey watched him approach an alleyway and then come back with two scared coolies in the shafts of two dusty rickshaws.

"Stow your cargo," said Mitchell, "and mount rickshaw."

"Aye, aye, sir," said Toughey with enthusiasm. He thumped the keg to the footboards and clambered in.

The two big coolies failed to understand anything about this. The two men in green uniforms were certainly white and therefore not Japanese, but what were white men in green uniforms doing in shattered Liaochow?

24

The two big coolies failed to understand anything about this.
The two men in green uniforms were certainly white and
therefore not Japanese, but what were white men
in green uniforms doing in shattered Liaochow?

Mitchell barked a string of Chinese commands and the coolies bent their backs and trotted off. Toughey sat back and viewed the scenery.

"This ain't bad," said Toughey. "Why the hell hasn't a landing party thought of this before? Say, do you suppose Davis would let me stow this guy away for future reference?"

Mitchell stretched out his long legs and lay back. "I don't know how long this is going to last, but while it does, it's the cat's."

The rickshaws rolled to the slap of bare feet. The big North Chinese were as tireless as a team of Clydes. The muscles in their glistening backs rippled and they trotted with the rhythm of metronomes.

The plains behind the city stretched out endlessly in all directions, strewn at intervals with the debris of war. The rear-guard action of the departing Chinese had not been without its casualties. Dogs and pigs wandered aimlessly through the fields. Occasionally the Marines passed a peasant sitting with head in hands beside the road, looking up bleakly and blankly at the strange foreign devils.

All went well for many kilometers and then the growing rumble of shellfire became very plain. It was five o'clock in the afternoon but the sun had long been hidden in the war-thickened air, and it was now twilight.

Rounding a curve in the road, they came upon the rear of the still-fighting Japanese army.

A cluster of huts, dwarfed by stacks of war supplies, was peopled by the soldiers in mustard.

Magically, a cordon of Japanese troops stretched with glittering bayonets before them.

"Halt," said Mitchell, rather belatedly as the coolies had already stopped in shivering dismay.

A *taii*, gaudy with red bands, stepped forward and snapped, *"Doko e yuku!"*

"What's he talkin' about?" growled Toughey.

"That's one lingo I don't sling," said Mitchell.

Toughey snorted. "Looks like an organ grinder's monkey, damned if he don't!"

"Ah," bristled the Japanese staff lieutenant, "so I look like a monkey, eh?"

"Yeah," said Toughey, feebly.

"Shut up," said Mitchell. "Lieutenant, you will please remove your troops from across the road in order that we may pass."

"Pass? So you wish to pass? And where do you think you are going?" The lieutenant's black brows lifted in mock surprise. "Perhaps you are carrying messages to the Chinese, eh? Perhaps you have contraband of war there, eh? No, no, it is impossible that you pass."

Mitchell stepped out of the rickshaw. Standing very straight-backed, he was head and shoulders above the lieutenant.

"Sir," said Mitchell, carefully, "I am Gunnery Sergeant James Mitchell of the United States Marines, in command of a landing party from the cruiser *Miami* of the Asiatic Station. My destination is the United States Consulate at Shunkien. You will please remove your troops instantly."

27

The lieutenant carried a little stick and he tried to tie it into knots. "A sergeant! A sergeant and you dare speak to a ranking officer in this manner? How dare—"

"Get this," said Mitchell. "A private in the United States Marines would rank an admiral in the Japanese Navy. Unless you order your troops to retire instantly, I shall be forced to report interference with the duties and operations of a landing party on a peaceful mission. Of course, if you wish to make an incident of this . . ."

The Japanese lieutenant was quite beyond speech. The infuriating lack of diplomacy in this American was enough to make his ancestors shriek in dismay.

Abruptly the lieutenant wheeled and scurried into a hut nearby. He was gone for some time.

"Maybe I hadn't ought to have said that," said Mitchell. "But he made me sore."

"Aw, what the hell," said Toughey. "You'n me could go a long ways toward cleanin' up this batch of ——."

The coolies were sweating terribly even though they had stopped working. They kept casting their eyes on the back trail.

Presently, the lieutenant appeared in the doorway and jerked his thumb at Mitchell, and Mitchell followed him into the presence of a very Buddha of a staff officer who sat in the middle of a meal big enough to feed half his army.

"This is the fellow," said the staff officer. "Quick, where are your diplomatic passports?"

Mitchell was very prompt. He pulled back his overcoat collar and displayed the globe and eagle and anchor on his lapel. "There is my passport, sir." He reached into his pocket

28

and brought out a sheaf of onionskin paper. "And here are my orders."

The staff officer wiped his hands on his tunic and took the orders. He mumbled over them for some time and then laid them down on his desk. "Very good. These are perfectly in order. You may proceed."

Mitchell held out his hand. "My orders, please."

"Ah, no. I can, of course, give you a receipt for them, but I am afraid that these will have to remain here as well as your coolies. We can allow no Chinese to pass through our lines and I see no mention of them here."

Mitchell's hand rested on the smoothly polished flap of his holster. He glanced around and saw that two sentries were very alert by the door.

He began to argue. But the staff officer was very polite, smiled and steadily shook his head in the negative.

There was a certain responsibility, said the staff officer, in letting two Marines through the lines. Without these papers to show in case of accident, the staff officer was sorry but he could not let the Marines continue.

And finally, fuming but baffled, Mitchell went back to the rickshaws.

"Get out," ordered Mitchell.

Toughey groaned and got out. He put the rifle across his back and the keg on his shoulder and stood waiting for Mitchell to lead him on.

Mitchell took two silver dollars of his expense money and gave it to the Chinese coolies. They bit the silver and made it ring and then started to turn around to head back for Liaochow.

Mitchell jerked his head at Toughey. "March."

The cordon opened up and they passed through, trudging up the dark roadway with the rumble of guns a steady concussion in their ears.

Behind them two pistol shots were sharp in the darkness.

Toughey gave Mitchell a quick look and said, "The dirty sons!"

Mitchell did not look back. He seemed to be watching a line of far-off flames which leaped redly into the sky.

Chapter Five

A dark and muttering midnight found Mitchell and Toughey slogging southwest with the din of war blazing all along the northern horizon. They had succeeded in skirting the main point of contention between the Japanese advance guard and the Chinese rear guard and had crossed the disrupted bed of the northwest-running railroad.

The sight of the blasted rails had been very discouraging to Toughey, as the last time he had had contact with them he had been riding a comfortable cushion.

They stumbled into a river bottom and for an hour poked into the huts along the banks to find a man who could find them a boat. Their luck held and soon they struck a roadway on the other side.

Toughey put the keg down and began to kick it along the uneven surface, occasionally swearing and rolling it up out of a ditch after a particularly hard boot.

"I'll take it any time," said Mitchell.

"Aw, what's the matter? You think I'm fallin' apart or something? I may have my twenty years in, but I've—"

"I was only trying to spell you," said Mitchell. "Chengchu is a mile or two ahead, if I remember this country. We'll try to get some rations there and maybe dig in for a few hours. We've made about twenty-five miles."

"A hundred and seventy-five to go," said Toughey and then, despite the bad meter, began to bawl, "A hundred and seventy-five miles to go, boys, a hundred and seventy-five miles to go. We'll walk a while and rest a while when we've a hundred and seventy-four miles to go. A hundred and seventy-four miles to go, boys, a hundred and seventy-four miles to go. We'll walk a while and rest a while when we've a hundred and seventy-three miles to go. A hundred and seventy-three miles to go, boys, a hundred and seventy-three miles to go. We'll walk a while and—"

They both stopped.

Up ahead there rose a sound which might have been a binding machine or a riveting hammer or a kid running a big stick along a picket fence.

Scarlet tongues of fire were stabbing the ebon sky and a rosy glow marked the place where Chengchu once had been.

The sound, which might have been a signal clacker and wasn't, stopped and then started up again.

"Somebody is having a party," said Mitchell dryly.

Toughey looked to his commanding officer and then rolled the keg back until it was up against his leg. He took his rifle off his back and checked the magazine.

Brisk hoofbeats sounded ahead. Mitchell grabbed Toughey's arm and Toughey grabbed the keg and they rolled off the road into a muddy ditch.

A squadron of Japanese cavalry rocketed by, heading east. Against the stars Mitchell saw two empty saddles. Something black was hanging down from one, bouncing as it hit rough spots in the road.

"Chinese troops ahead," said Mitchell. "We've come up with their wing." He wondered a moment about the possibility of nervous sentries and then turned to Toughey. "Come on."

Toughey shouldered the keg and they stepped back up on the road to proceed short distances at a time, to stop and listen intently.

The town grew larger and the surrounding plain began to glow eerily from the light of the flaming town. Beneath the smoke, lorries were moving out, going west.

Expecting momentarily to be greeted by the machine gunner, they left the road and began to circle to the left. They stumbled from time to time over the debris of a battle so recent that the acrid fumes of smokeless powder still hung in the dust. Evidently the Japanese had been rolled back at this point but had bulged the Chinese center until the troops in Chengchu were in danger of being flanked.

Mitchell appreciated this in a vague way. He surmised that another Japanese army was coming up from the south and that another Chinese army was trying to stop its progress. The only thing he knew clearly was that this was a bewildering hodgepodge of yellow men with rifles.

The last lorry rumbled out of sight ahead of them and a squadron of Chinese troopers were momentarily silhouetted against the flames of a burning warehouse. All outposts were evidently drawn in and the cavalry was on the scout.

Mitchell warily approached the end of a street. They were tired and hungry and they read little likelihood of food in this gutted village. But Mitchell knew better than to go stumbling across the plains in darkness with cavalry nervously outriding.

33

The blasted houses presented an ugly sight. A Chinese soldier hung head down out of a window, fingertips touching the ground. An old woman was sprawled in the gutter, almost covered by the burst bag of possessions she had tried to save. A wounded and deserted Chinese soldier hitched himself slowly around the mounds in the street, leaving a squirming trail in the dust like a snake's, inching himself west after the departing lorries.

Ahead, a cavalry patrol had stopped before the only building in town which had remained intact. It was the local hotel and before it stood an American car.

Mitchell called a halt and Toughey put down the keg with a weary thump.

"We better not run into that," said Mitchell, pointing ahead at the clustered horsemen.

Toughey sat down on the keg and planted his rifle butt in the dirt.

"Wonder what they're up to," said Mitchell. "If they'll clear out, that car might be in running condition."

"Car?" said Toughey, brightening.

Three of the Chinese were dismounted and inside. They came out now, leading a girl in a blue swagger coat.

At first Mitchell thought she was Chinese and then by the flaring flames across the street he saw her face. She was white!

She threw the three soldiers away from her. An officer was pouring a tirade of Chinese into her stubborn ears. She stood defiantly before them, glaring at them.

"Clear out!" she shouted at them. "Beat it! Leave me alone!"

The officer made a movement with his hand and the three soldiers strove to lay hands on her again. But she was too swift for that. She beat at their faces with her bare hands. Her hat came off and her platinum hair streamed down over her shoulders.

She whirled and ran, the Chinese following. Ahead of her she saw Mitchell and Toughey and, taking them for more Chinese, tried to turn and double back.

The three troopers were upon her instantly, seizing her arms.

Mitchell paced forward. The first man thought that an artillery shell had hit him. The second thought not at all. The third stood aghast, slack-armed, backing up. Behind him an arm sprang into being, whirled him around. Toughey gave him a solid punch in the chest which sent him rolling up against the corner of the hotel.

The girl was facing Mitchell. Her mouth was open in amazement and her bright blue eyes were very wide, made wider by mascara. "F'gawd sakes!" she gulped. "Th' *Marines*!"

"Yes'm," said Mitchell. "Will that car run?"

"Sure. How did you think I got here?"

"Oh, boy," said Toughey, hugging his rifle to port and whirling to face the troopers.

The Chinese officer, his voice loud and shrill, advanced upon them. Behind him he knew that every carbine in his squadron was unlimbered.

Mitchell stepped forward to meet him. They talked swiftly and angrily.

"Where's the rest of you guys?" demanded the girl.

35

"Ain't two of us enough?" said Toughey out of the side of his face.

"That guy slings the lingo, don't he?" said the girl.

"Yeah," said Toughey. "He slings the lingo and I sling the lead. This ain't no tea party, sister."

"You're tellin' me?"

Mitchell's height was taut. His lean, tan face was stiff and the Chinese rapid-fired out of his mouth like a 1917 Browning.

"He sounds like a native," said the girl. "How come?"

"His pa was a missionary around here once."

She seemed to find this very funny and Toughey growled, "Shut up. We ain't out of this yet by a hell of a ways."

Mitchell was walking straight into the officer, and the Chinese, faced with such an irresistible force, could do nothing but give ground. Toughey and the girl moved up in Mitchell's wake, Toughey kicking the keg along.

Mitchell turned. "He says everybody has got to get out of this area. He says he was just trying to make you move along. You've got to go someplace but he doesn't know where and neither do I. What are we going to do with you?"

"Do you have to do anything with me?" said the girl.

"This is your car, isn't it?" said Mitchell.

"In a way."

"Then get into it."

The girl got in and Toughey lifted the keg after her. The uncertain troopers sat their nervous horses, rifles in hand. One of them pulled slowly out of the group and rode around in back of the hotel. He was gone for some time and when he came back, Mitchell was sliding under the wheel of the car.

The trooper yelled to the officer and the officer whirled to shout at his men.

Mitchell stepped off the clutch and on the gas. The car shot away. The troopers surged ahead. A carbine banged and glass showered out of a window.

Toughey jabbed the glass out of the back. He fired and worked his bolt and fired again.

"And a bull's-eye at one o'clock," said Toughey. "And another bull's-eye at one o'clock. Hey, slow up, you're spoilin' my aim!"

Mitchell stepped on the throttle and slewed the car around the end of the street and down another. Ahead they could see the lorries but the road forked to the left and they raced in that direction.

After ten minutes of speed, Mitchell eased up. "Who the hell ordered you to fire?"

"Huh?" said Toughey.

"I said who the hell told you to shoot?"

"Well, for Christ's sake!" wailed Toughey. "They was almost ridin' over the top of the car! I had to do something, didn't I?"

"The next time you get ideas," said Mitchell, "tell me first. Did you hit anybody?"

"Well . . . no. You was hittin' the bumps so hard I couldn't even get a squint through the peep. I was just guessin'."

Mitchell sighed with relief but he did not relent. "As long as I'm in command of this landin' party, there's going to be a minimum of provocation for incidents, see? We aren't trying to fight this war, we're trying to get to Shunkien."

Toughey subsided and was gloomy for almost a minute. Then he perked up and took off his cap and selected a cigarette and a match and lit up.

The girl was staring sideways at Mitchell with some wonder. "What are you talking about, 'landing party'? There's only two of you."

Mitchell's dignity was hurt. "That don't make any difference. We're ashore, aren't we? And we're on duty, aren't we? What are you doing running around China alone?"

"I wasn't alone. I had a driver but he beat it. Listen, Captain—"

"I'm not a captain. I'm a gunnery sergeant."

"That's higher'n a captain," added Toughey from the rear seat.

"Oh," said the girl, disappointed. She looked with some distrust at Mitchell and then edged a little toward the door.

"What are you doing running around here?" persisted Mitchell.

She scowled a little thoughtfully and then looked at him. "My father is a millionaire and he owns a lot of land near here and the troops tried to steal everything. They kidnaped my father but I managed to get away and ran into a battle this afternoon."

Mitchell looked at her for an instant. He saw the platinum hair and the jaunty little hat which had a brim to it like a jockey's and the mascara and the powder and the rouge. He did not object to any of these things. In fact he rather favored them. But he noted them all the same.

"Gee, a millionaire?" said Toughey.

"Sure, and if you boys would put me someplace where there wasn't a war on, he'd make it worth your while. Plenty. Maybe a couple hundred dollars apiece."

Mitchell smiled quietly to himself and kept driving.

"Hell, lady," said Toughey, "we're goin' to Shunkien and we got—"

"Shut up," said Mitchell. "I'm sorry, but you got to go with us, lady, no matter where we're going, unless you want that incident back there repeated."

"How come everybody got so mad all of a sudden?" said Toughey.

"Yeah, what was that all about?" said the girl.

"Oh, I told him we were the advance guard of a company and he tried to stall me. He was raising the dickens with you because he thought he could take some cash off of you.

The rest was just a stall, like my regiment of Marines. And when that trooper saw the plain was empty behind us, they got soured, that's all. Most of these fellows are fifty percent patriot and fifty percent brigand."

"Gee, you talk elegant sometimes," said the girl.

Mitchell favored her with a grin, but the light on his face was only that from the instrument panel and she read it wrong. She edged further away from him and looked uncomfortable.

"Now if this buggy will only hold out," said Toughey, "we'll get to Shunkien in style."

And a few minutes later, the engine began to wheeze and gasp and then it stopped and the night was very still.

Mitchell looked into the gas tank and rocked the car. "Dry," he announced. "Unload."

Toughey got down and swung the keg up on his shoulder once more, letting out a weary, hungry groan. The girl looked scared.

"Gee, we got to walk?" she said, staring at the rough road which fanned out before the headlights.

Mitchell looked at her feet and saw the extreme French heels she wore.

"Sure we got to walk," said Mitchell. "Unless you want to stay here."

Hurriedly she fell in between them, striving to lengthen her stride in spite of her tight skirt.

The headlights fell behind them and finally vanished. The heavy tread of Marine shoes was cut by the triphammer beat of the French heels.

Chapter Six

NEAR dawn, Mitchell saw a cluster of mean huts, squat and but half seen in the uncertain light.

"Halt," said Mitchell, advancing alone, hand resting on the polished flap of his holster.

Toughey put down the keg with a prompt thump and was about to sink upon it when he recalled himself. "Have a seat, sister?"

She was too tired to answer. She sank down and sat there motionless, panting for a long while. She could hear Mitchell's solid footsteps somewhere in the chill gloom ahead.

Toughey took off his cap, selected a cigarette and started to light it when he remembered himself again. He extended the cap upside down to the girl. "Have a smoke?"

"You saved m'life," she said huskily and took a drag so deep that Toughey thought she never would exhale. He let out his own breath when she let out hers.

It seemed to revive her as she crossed her legs and took her right foot in both hands. The slipper lay tipped over in the dirt as though it was too tired to stand up.

"How long do we have to keep this up?"

"'Nother hundred and sixty-five miles," said Toughey.

"Y'mean we have to *walk?*"

"Unless the Japanese give us a general's car and a military escort—which ain't likely to happen. You're lucky. That damned keg gets a pound heavier every thousand yards and it's up to a ton and a half by now."

"What's in it?"

"Damned if I know," said Toughey disinterestedly.

"Maybe we can rest here a day or so."

"No sir. We got to be in Shunkien by Saturday and if we want to make it, the rests are gonna be few and far between."

She sighed and sought solace in the smoke, eyeing Toughey. His big, battered face with its broken nose and lopsided jaw interested her. She'd never seen a man as big as Toughey.

"You're a funny duck," she decided.

"Who?"

"You. Somebody tells you to deliver a keg to a town two hundred miles away and you take it without even knowing what's in it. Does *he* know?"

"Don't think so. Why should we know what's in it?"

"Maybe if I asked him real nice, he'd stick around until some of this swelling gets out of my dogs. Do you suppose he would?"

"Him?" said Toughey, incredulous. "Orders is orders!" Toughey scratched his stubbly jaw. "Only one thing ever stops Jimmy Mitchell and that's tanglefoot."

"What?"

"Redeye. Panther sweat. Th' demon rum. As long as he can keep away from the stuff, he'd keep goin' if he was dead."

"Y'mean he's a booze fighter?"

"Yeah. He can't stop. Been that way ever since he got into the service. Gunnery sergeant one minute and a PFC the next. Likker sure makes a rolly-coaster out of livin' for the sarge."

"Never saw a drunk yet without some reason for drinkin'.."

Mitchell's voice came to them out of the swimming morning mist and they followed the sound to find him standing in the doorway of a hut. Now and then he wiped his hands on his overcoat.

"Nobody here," said Mitchell. "They cleared out and left some beans and potatoes. Get a fire going, Toughey, and we'll eat."

"You going to stop here and sleep?" begged the girl, limping up.

"For about three hours. We only made about thirty-five miles yesterday and we should have made fifty. If we hadn't had to detour . . ."

Toughey had gone into a back room in search of firewood and had left the building by the rear door. He appeared at the front now.

"Hey, Sarge, there's a couple—"

"Shut up," said Mitchell. "Get some wood and make a fire. Are you deaf or what?"

"But there's—"

"Goddammit!" barked Mitchell. "Can't you follow a simple order like that? Get some wood and build a fire!"

"Okay," said Toughey, backing out.

43

An hour later they had finished their meal. The day was growing yellow outside the glassless windows. Inside the room, just before the door, were a number of small pits all in a line.

Mitchell spread his coat and blanket for the girl.

"Where you going to sleep?" she said quickly.

"Outside. One of us will have to keep watch and that leaves an extra blanket. You better get what shut-eye you can, lady. We'll be falling in in a few hours."

"Listen, mister, ain't there a chance of stayin' here a little longer? I could sleep a year and still be short on rest."

"Nope. Sorry, but we've got to get to Shunkien."

"But why? A couple Marines won't make any difference more or less in that town."

"Maybe not," said Mitchell. "But I got my orders."

"Ain't you scared of bein' shot in some of this fightin' around here?"

"Sure, but it's my business to see that we aren't. Now get some sleep."

"And you won't change your mind?"

"Sorry."

She sat up suddenly and cried, "You're not sorry or anything of the kind. I think you're just trying to get rid of me by walkin' my legs off. Who the hell do you think I am?"

"I said get some sleep," said Mitchell. "If you don't, that's your hard luck. If you can't take it and if you'd rather stay here alone . . ."

"No. Wait a minute. I didn't mean to get mad. Honest."

Mitchell smiled at her and instantly she chilled. "G'wan. How can I follow your orders with you standin' there grinnin' at me?"

Mitchell went outside and found Toughey dozing in a patch of cold sunlight. Toughey woke up instantly.

"Go ahead and cork off," said Mitchell. "I'll keep a lookout for an hour and then let you have it."

"Hey," said Toughey, aggrieved, "what's the idea tellin' me to pipe down a while ago? I was just tryin' to say that there's a couple Japanese stiffs around the corner there all shot to hell with machine-gun bullets."

"Sure, that was all you had to say. Who do you think put them there?"

"You?" gaped Toughey.

"You wouldn't want that girl to fall over a couple stiffs, would you?"

Toughey's battered face lighted up. "Gee, that's so. No wonder they made you a sergeant."

"Can the wisecracks," said Mitchell, moving off. He sat down against the wall and pulled a small purse out of his blouse. He opened it up and took out a bountiful store of cosmetics and then some papers.

Toughey was interested immediately. "What's that?"

"Pipe down," said Mitchell with a glance at the wall behind him.

"You got her pocketbook," said Toughey.

"Sure I have. She thought she left it in the car. Think I want to convoy a spy halfway across China?"

"A spy?" gaped Toughey. "Say, that's right. That millionaire story did sound kind of phony now that I come to think of it. Hell, Sarge, maybe she's just usin' us to—"

"Pipe down. Do you want her to hear you?"

Mitchell ran through the papers and spread one out. It was a newspaper clipping which said that Dawn LeMontraine, world's most famous fan dancer, had appeared in Shanghai with great success. Her next engagement was to be Tientsin. The dateline was May third, many months before. The picture was that of the girl.

"A fan dancer!" grinned Toughey. "Well, for gawd's sake! A fan dancer!"

"Think of that," said Mitchell acidly. "Now get some sleep or I'll give you something to make you snore."

"Whatcha so mad about?" said Toughey.

"Listen," said Mitchell, carefully, "if you don't start snappin' into it, I'll hold out ten days' pay. Understand?"

Toughey was so worried that he went to sleep the instant he sat back against the wall.

For a long time, Mitchell listened to his snores. At length he got up and paced nervously around the huts, looking out into the plains for cavalry and spotting occasional bombers which flew along the horizon.

Now that he was left to himself, he knew how tired he had been made by the nervous strain. His mouth and throat felt raw and he was a little sick to his stomach.

Shunkien was so very far away and the dull, muttering thunder in the air said that the way was hard.

46

Mitchell came back to his pack, thinking he might refresh himself with a shave. The bulge of the bottle was under his hand. Unwillingly he unbuckled it and read the label.

His throat was so dry and his mouth was so parched. . . . *Canadian Whisky. Five Years Old. One Quart.* Just one drink wouldn't do any harm. Just one drink . . . But if he took that drink he would finish the bottle. He knew he would.

And still . . . Just one, small drink . . .

His mouth was set as he forced himself to put the bottle back. He padded it so that he could not feel the sharp corners.

He had won. He ought to throw the damned thing up against the wall, but he could not.

Wearily he asked himself, would he win next time?

Shunkien was so very far away!

Chapter Seven

A T noon Wednesday, two regiments of Chinese infantry and three batteries of artillery reinforced the fragments defending Shunkien. A half-hour later their howitzers began to wham in the streets, pounding the Japanese on the ridge and succeeding in blasting two tanks which had sought to blast the gates.

At one, Japanese bombers were on their way and at exactly two-thirty-five Shunkien was again mauled from the air.

Jackson, his white hair standing straight up on his head and his thin hands trembling, bent over his radio operator's desk. "Some of the women are getting hysterical, Billy. Get the USS *Miami,* if you can, and find out what's been done."

The youth laid his cigarette on the edge of his desk and leaned through the smoke to throw the starter switch on his auxiliary generator.

Jackson watched him intently, jumping when a bomb exploded close enough to make the floor shake. The machinery salesman, red face glistening, touched his arm.

"Mr. Jackson," said the salesman, "I been checking over the supplies like you told me and I can't find much but ham. If you'd let me and Stevens slide out, maybe we could scare up a Chinese willing to sell us some supplies. I . . . I haven't got much use for ham, Mr. Jackson."

"We haven't any money," said Jackson tiredly.

"I thought of that. A lot of us have got banker's checks. I've got five hundred and it's at your disposal."

"You don't know these Chinese," said Jackson. "Knowing they would be looted no matter who won, most of the bankers have fled or hidden their money. And back here, nothing buys but gold at a time like this."

"Shucks, Mr. Jackson, you aren't very likely to find any gold on a bunch of *Americans* these days. Maybe I could jawbone a few crates of canned goods. There was a store a couple blocks from here."

"I can't allow it, sir," said Jackson.

"But why not?"

"In the first place, the attempt would fail. In the second place . . . well . . . ah . . . the fact is . . ."

"Say, something's eating you and the doc. What is it? I don't see anything wrong with getting out for a spell. I'm not afraid of these bombs. I'm going to try anyhow."

"No, no!" said Jackson swiftly. He pulled the rotund salesman over into the corner. "You see . . . the fact is . . . a couple of the native boys report . . . well . . . cholera."

"I've had a cholera shot," said the salesman. "I'm not scared of *that*. It's just that I don't care much for ham. You see . . ."

"You've had a cholera shot, true. All of us have had *one*. But you see . . . You won't spread this?"

"Of course not!" said the salesman indignantly.

"Epidemic Asiatic cholera is . . . well . . . very violent. And in an exposed area, it is necessary to have a secondary shot before one is immune. Otherwise, if cholera begins to spread inside here . . ."

"Hell, ain't we boiling our water?"

"Certainly. But you see, food, clothing, the very air we breathe, is likely to be infected. If we stay here we may be safe but if one of us comes in contact with the streets and the . . . well, you understand, sir."

"Aw, you're gettin' serious about it. What's cholera but a bellyache, huh?"

"Asiatic cholera," said Jackson with dignity, "is a 'bellyache' bad enough to kill a man in a day. The first stages are quite awful enough and are followed with agonizing cramps in the legs and stomach. The victim turns blue and is very cold and he can only speak in a hoarse whisper. And then, in an hour or two, he dies and so violent is the disease that the body rises in temperature after the death. I have been in epidemic areas, sir, and I know that these hundred and sixteen Americans would die in a matter of a day or two after exposure."

The salesman ran his finger under his collar. "I . . . I didn't know it was that bad!"

"You will therefore refrain from foraging on your own," said Jackson, triumphantly.

"You bet," said the salesman shakily. "But wait. We haven't got much food left! In a couple days, we'll be starving if we can't leave here!"

"We can't leave here," said Jackson, "but I think the serum for the second shots will be here by Saturday. If we then have money, we will be as safe as can be expected in a battle area."

The salesman went away, muttering to himself and staring popeyed straight ahead. His hands were running over his stomach as though already detecting the first symptoms.

The radio operator turned. "I had the *Miami*, sir. She's on her way back to Shanghai. Here is the message."

Jackson grabbed his decoding book and started to work. The doctor stared over his shoulder with bated breath, straining his eyes to read the letters which began to string out.

Finally the consul had it!

JACKSON
UNITED STATES CONSUL SHUNKIEN

BE ADVISED THAT TWENTY-FIVE THOUSAND DOLLARS IN BRITISH GOLD IS BEING CONVEYED TO YOU AND YOUR REQUIRED MEDICAL SUPPLIES. GUNNERY SERGEANT JAMES MITCHELL IS UNDER ORDERS TO REPORT TO YOU NOT LATER THAN SATURDAY.

V. G. BLACKSTONE CAPT. USN
COMMANDING
USS *MIAMI*

The consul trembled as he handed the message to the doctor but that worthy had already read it and his invisible eyes were glowing.

"Looks easy enough," said the doctor. "Even if a few do get it, the serum will be here in time. It's certain we can't leave here at all unless we *do* get it."

"Yes," whispered Jackson, feeling the throb of the floor beneath his feet as another aerial bomb blammed into Shunkien. "Yes, it looks easy. Only two major offensives and two hundred miles of war-gutted China between here and Liaochow."

Chapter Eight

DUSK was seeping across the barren hills. The wide and fertile plains below were already merged into a deep pool of ink. To the north, scattered mountaintops were a deep rose, a color to match the patch of unsteady light on the southern horizon—which might be artillery or a burning town. A rumble like summer thunder pulsed in the air.

Mitchell turned a climbing curve in the rutted highway and stopped, stepping back. He faced about.

"We crossed a stream a hundred yards back. Double time!"

"What?" said the girl. "Y'mean we got to go back and then walk *up* again?"

Mitchell was bearing down upon her as though he would run over her if she did not move. She turned and walked.

Toughey set the old man of the sea down and let it roll. Gravity was kind. The keg teetered off a bridge and dropped five feet to the almost dry creek bed.

"Under the bridge," said Mitchell. "Quick!"

Toughey hauled the keg into the gloom, upended it and waited for the girl to seat herself. But she had other ideas. She perched herself on a rock beside a pool of water and took off what was left of her slippers. With a voluptuous sigh of pure pleasure, she slid her feet into the cool water.

"What's up?" said Toughey, turning his sling and sliding his left arm into it. He worked his bolt and stood facing the outside edge of the bridge.

"About two hundred Chinese cavalry," replied Mitchell. "They're coming this way. Maybe we'll be lucky enough to have them pass up this stream for a watering place."

"Would they do anything to us?" said the girl.

"We can't take that chance," said Mitchell. "Without orders, anything is liable to happen."

"I thought you had orders."

He shook his head. "I had to give them up at the first Japanese PC we hit."

The clatter of hoofs, the clink of sabers and the creak of leather came from afar, growing louder. Toughey took his arm out of the sling and fixed his bayonet. Mitchell unbuckled the flap of his holster.

The bridge trembled and the amplified sound was deafening. Dust and stones showered down on either side for an interminable time. Finally the rear guard was over and gone and the hoofbeats were swallowed by distance.

Toughey unfixed his bayonet, slung his rifle across his back, took off his cap and selected a cigarette. He sat down on the keg, puffing thoughtfully.

Mitchell went up on the road and looked down the hill, but it was now much too dark below to see anything. He came back.

"We might as well eat before we go on."

"Go on?" said the girl faintly. "Gosh, don't you guys ever

get tired? Listen, maybe a moon will come up later on. Let's take a little shut-eye and then hike about mid—"

"If you don't mind," said Mitchell mildly, "I'll make our plans."

"I was thinking," she protested, "that if there was two hundred cavalry, there might be more along the road."

"That's a chance we've got to take," said Mitchell. "We can find other places to duck."

He slid his pack off his shoulders and she watched for him to flex his arms and stretch. But he didn't. He acted as though the pack weighed a pound and no more. Disappointed, she watched him bring forth some of the provender he had foraged along the way—some peanuts and a few chunks of bread.

They fell to on the chow and cleaned it up. The girl was silent as she ate but as soon as she had finished, it was plain that she had been spending her time in thought.

"Listen, mister," she said, "if you was to take me to the nearest point out, my old man could make it worth your while. Did I tell you he was the soybean king?"

"No," said Mitchell. "Is he?"

"Sure. He can write his check for a million any old day. Now if you boys would just quit this everlasting march, march, march and put me someplace where I could be taken care of—"

"Save it," said Mitchell. "There's no such place. I realize your feet are practically on the ground but we can't slow down and still make Shunkien by Saturday. Here it is Wednesday night and we've only got tomorrow and Friday to make most of our time."

"Maybe you can get a car someplace. I'm telling you, mister, if my old man—"

"Please," said Mitchell.

"Maybe you don't think my old man *is* the soybean king," she said indignantly.

"No, I don't," replied Mitchell.

She was shocked. "You mean you don't believe me?"

"I mean just that. Quit pulling the line. You're Dawn LeMontraine, the fan dancer."

"How . . . how did you find that out?"

"You left your purse in the car, and now that I've told you, you can have it back." He gave it to her and her fingers were eager as she opened it.

She powdered her nose and rouged her lips and made herself very attractive. Mitchell, looking at her, forgot himself for a moment.

"I'm sorry I pulled that gag," she said unabashed. "Thanks for rescuing my war paint. I felt down without it."

Mitchell grinned at her and she froze up immediately. Hurriedly she began to pull on her stockings.

"Okay, Marine. Keep your distance."

"Look here," said Mitchell. "You've got me all wrong. What was the idea of telling me that whopper in the first place?"

She looked at him resentfully. "I knew what I was doing. I suppose I should have come right out and said I was what I am. I know Marines by reputation. And—"

"That's interesting," said Mitchell. "Even if not true."

"Well, I got to take care of myself, haven't I?"

He merely looked at her.

But she was tired and the food had not been good and she wanted to take a hot bath and then sleep forever and then ride the rest of her life.

She stopped putting on her slippers and put her head down in her hands and her platinum hair cascaded over her knees. Her shoulders shook.

Mitchell knew it was his fault. He moved closer to her and put his hand on her shoulder to tell her he was sorry.

She whipped away from him and stood up, backing angrily. "See? What did I tell you? I let down my guard and you try to make a pass at me. Gee, guy," and the tears were big in her blue eyes, "can't you be square?"

"I was just—"

"Sure. Sure. That's what they all say!" She drew herself up. "Get this, Marine. I'm a one-man woman, and I haven't met him yet. Am I understood?"

Mitchell was sliding into his pack again. He motioned at Toughey to come on and Toughey shouldered the keg.

She put on her wrecks of slippers and followed them back to the inky road, falling in between them and marching.

For an hour and four miles, not a word was said. And then Mitchell spoke.

"What's your real name?"

"Goldy Brown. And if you laugh, I'll kill you."

"Okay, Goldy."

Chapter Nine

A T two o'clock in the morning, human life is at its lowest ebb—and it must have been close to that dark and eerie hour when Goldy dropped down on a milestone and refused to go on.

Mitchell looked at her for a long time. "You mean you don't care whether we leave you or not?"

"No, I don't care," she wept. "Keep going. I don't care what happens to me, but for God's sake don't make me go on!"

Mitchell tried to pull her to her feet.

"Leave me alone!" she whimpered. "You don't care what happens to me! All you can think about is your orders. To hell with your orders! They don't include me." She subsided, slumping wearily, every muscle in her body screaming for rest. There was less than a shred left of her slippers.

Mitchell lighted a match to look at her and by its jerky glow, her face was haggard. He dropped it and it glowed in the black road.

"Get up!" said Mitchell, his voice sharp and hard. "Get up and walk. I didn't ask you to stay with us and now that you are, you'll carry on. Get up!"

She did not move. He grabbed her arm and jerked her to her feet. She sagged away from him and he angrily straightened her up. Half dragging her, he forced her on up the road. Staggering, Toughey limped after them.

Mechanically then, she was again walking, too numb with fatigue to mind the pain anymore. And when she faltered, Mitchell's harsh voice whipped her on.

After a racked eternity, Mitchell called a halt. Toughey and the girl sat down in the road, dimly aware of the dawn which had begun to spread its crimson flood across the plains. Mitchell was gone for some time and at last Toughey perked up enough to light himself a cigarette and look around. He saw Mitchell coming back. Beyond Mitchell there was a sandbagged wall, sprawled bodies and a broken, smoking gun carriage.

Mitchell sank down beside Goldy. He had three pairs of felt shoes under his arm and, one by one, he held their soles to her feet. The smallest pair fitted her.

Mitchell stood up. "We're several miles to the north of our course."

"Lost?" said Toughey.

"No. We're detouring toward Yin-Meng and if we're lucky we can get a car there."

"A car?" said Goldy huskily.

"How?" demanded Toughey.

"March," said Mitchell.

They moved on through the smoky birth of day and as they progressed, the countryside became more and more littered with the debris of war. Mitchell's hopes sank in inverse ratio. This, then, had been the scene of the far-off battle they had heard. Somewhere around them armies were on the march. Somewhere ahead were the hurdles of both Chinese and Japanese PCs.

Directly ahead, crushed by shells into a river bank, was Yin-Meng.

A straggling line of refugees dragged dismally down the broken road, pushing wheelbarrows, bending their backs under children and bedding, hauling unwilling animals. Even the dogs were silent.

The apathy on the Chinese faces was complete in its recognition of fate. The sad brown eyes were not even curious enough to examine the two men in olive green and the girl in the dusty blue swagger coat. Mitchell touched the arm of a shrunken old man.

The ancient looked up into the sergeant's haggard face. And then, miraculously, fear gave way to stunned surprise.

The ancient spoke gladly and Mitchell, his stubbly face cracking into a grin, replied.

For several minutes they spoke and then the old man began to shake his head and point into the west. And Mitchell shook his head and pointed east.

They parted, finally, and Goldy and Toughey got up and followed on.

"He looked like he knew you," said Toughey, reviving with the day.

"Sure," said Mitchell. "I haven't seen him since I left here fifteen years ago."

"You've been in this place before?"

"I was born in Yin-Meng," said Mitchell.

Toughey looked at the shattered town which grew larger ahead.

A walled set of stone buildings stood upon the river bank. Through the unhinged gates, trampled gardens could be seen. On the cobblestones within stood a limousine and beside it crouched a man who would have been a scarecrow if he had not been so fat.

His coattail was in shreds and his right pants leg was ripped from knee to ankle. His bald head glistened with sweat as he worked.

On the approach of the strange trio he stopped work and looked up, holding a monkey wrench uncertainly in his grease-smeared hand. Upon his long nose were perched a gold-rimmed pince-nez from which drooped a long black silk ribbon. One end of his clerical collar had become unfastened and stood out straight from the back of his neck. Mitchell marched through the gate, smiling faintly.

"Hello, Father."

The man gulped convulsively. He took off his pince-nez and gave them a violent polishing. He put them back and steadied them with his pudgy hand.

"James!" he exclaimed. He detached his gaze from the face of his son and stared at the uniform. "A Marine!"

"Father, I know you'll hardly consider my visit a social call and I'm in as much a hurry as you are. I want a car."

"Oh, my goodness!" wailed the Reverend Mitchell. "It can't

be done. Those Philistines have looted me! Positively looted me! I had nine cars and a station wagon and not one of them is left but this. And it won't run, James! It won't run!"

"Toughey," said Mitchell, crisply, "the monkey wrench."

Toughey advanced and followed his orders. He poked his broken nose under the hood and began to pry around.

"I must make the coast," said the agitated reverend. "There is nothing left. Nothing left! They've taken everything! Even my money. You'll help me make the coast, James? Of course you will!"

"I'll help you all I can," replied Mitchell. "Is there any food in the house?"

"Not a bite."

"Are you certain, Father?"

"Well, er . . . I had a few supplies. But I need them, James! It may be days before I can make Liaochow."

"It is more blessed to give than to receive," said Mitchell.

"Oh, yes, yes, yes. Yes, indeed, my boy. But really I haven't a tin to spare. They've looted me of everything! Everything!"

"Pardon me, Father," said Mitchell, going by. He reached into the tonneau and began to pull out corn willy and pears and potatoes and coffee.

Goldy was much recovered by the sight of the car and the glimpse of the food. She looked around her with some interest. "A mission, huh? This is a pretty swell layout you got here, Reverend."

"But they've looted it!" wailed the elder Mitchell. "It was the finest mission in the province and now look at it. Look at it!" Tears fogged his glasses and he took them off and shined them.

"When Toughey here said the sarge's old man was a missionary, I thought it was a big laugh, but I guess it's the straight goods."

The reverend looked at her with an uncomprehending frown. "What a strange language you speak, young lady. May I ask why you are touring about this country with my son?"

"Aw, it's out of the bag by now," said Goldy, sitting down on the running board and watching Mitchell vanish into one of the small stone houses. "I was on my way from Shanghai to Peking via the Tientsin-Pukow Railway when this war started up. Everybody said it would be over before it began so I sat down in Teng—after the rails were ripped up—and thought maybe I'd pick up some jack on the side. But the war got hot around Teng and I rented a car and driver to take me to Liaochow and . . . well . . . here I am."

"Extraordinary," said the reverend. "And you met my son? But tell me, how is it that an unescorted young lady would wander about China at such a time?"

"Unescorted? Are you tryin' to pull my leg?"

"Oh, no. Good gracious, no. I . . . ah . . . would never dream of such a thing. But why is it? Where are your parents?"

"In the Bronx, mister. In the Bronx."

"And they allowed you to . . ."

"Nix, Reverend. I've supported my old man since I could do a handstand on amateur night."

"A . . . a what?"

"Handstand. I'm a fan dancer."

"A *fan* dancer. My goodness. You mean you're a . . . a woman of the stage? A chorus girl?"

"No, I ain't a chorus girl. I do a solo."

"My, my, my. First he is a Marine and then he goes about with a dancer! I *knew* he wouldn't come to any good." This seemed to stiffen the reverend's spine and he waddled over and tapped Toughey on the shoulder.

"Are you having any luck, my man? I mean can you repair the thing?"

"I don't know. I'm undoing all you did," said Toughey ungraciously. "I ain't run into one of these wagons for twenty years. You ought to be able to get a lot of money for this as an antique, Reverend."

"Oh, I assure you it was my oldest car. When the troops came through here at midnight, they got it to run this far and could get it no further and . . . ah . . . I was never much a hand at machinery."

"You tellin' me?" said Toughey. "You was tryin' to screw the timer onto the carburetor. Now beat it and let me alone and maybe I'll be able to get into the guts of this thing."

"It's precisely a hundred and two miles to the coast," said the reverend, retreating. "We should be able to make it—"

"That's not news," cut in Goldy, staring down at her feet.

Mitchell was coming back with an armful of steaming kettles and the tools of attack.

"You mean you came from the coast?" said the reverend. "But where were you going?"

"Why, to . . . OUCH! Hey, Sarge, what the hell's the idea? Tryin' to bust my shins for me?"

"Sorry," said Mitchell. "Pipe down for chow, Toughey."

The reverend eyed the heaped plates with great misgivings and, watching Toughey stow away a warehouse of food, was so visibly affected that he had to wipe his glasses half a dozen times during the meal.

After he had stoked himself until he had to let out his belt a notch, Toughey renewed his attack on the car to learn at last that a battery cable had jarred loose.

He stood back and swabbed the grease from his hands and face with an already grimy handkerchief. He climbed up under the wheel and started the car. It ran with great smoothness.

With satisfaction radiating from him, he got down again and stowed the keg into the rear seat. "Who's drivin', Sarge?"

"I'll take the first trick," said Mitchell. "Are we all set, Father?"

"My boy, you have saved my life! We must get out of here before those troops come back."

The reverend got into the front seat, knowing of old that it was the smoothest riding. Goldy luxuriously stretched herself on the cushions and went to sleep abruptly in the middle of a yawn.

Toughey planted both feet on the keg, settled his enormous bulk, stood his rifle between his knees and was snoring before the car had even reached the gate.

Mitchell drove out between the pillars and turned into the road, heading west.

Until that turn, the reverend was most complacent.

Stories
from the
Golden Age
by L. Ron Hubbard

Join the Stories from the Golden Age Book Club Today!

Yes! Sign me up for the Book Club (*check one of the following*) and each month I will receive:

○ One paperback book at $9.95 a month.
○ Or, one unabridged audiobook CD at the cost of $9.95 a month.

Book Club members get FREE SHIPPING **and handling** (applies to US residents only).

Name   (please print)

If under 18, signature of guardian

Address

City   State   ZIP   Telephone

E-mail

You may sign up by doing any of the following:
1. To pay by credit card go online at www.goldenagestories.com
2. Call toll-free 1-877-842-5299 or fax this card in to 1-323-466-7817
3. Send in this card with a check for the first month
   payable to Galaxy Press

To get a FREE Stories from
the Golden Age catalog check here ○
and mail or fax in this card.

Thank you!

Subscribe today!
And get a FREE gift.

For details, go to www.goldenagestories.com

For an up-to-date listing of available titles visit www.goldenagestories.com
YOU CAN CANCEL AT ANY TIME AND RETURN THE BOOK AND AUDIO FOR A FULL REFUND.
Prices are set in US dollars only. For non-US residents, please call 1-323-466-7815 for pricing information or go to
www.goldenagestories.com. Terms, prices and conditions are subject to change. Subscription is subject to acceptance.

Stories from the Golden Age
by L. Ron Hubbard

BUSINESS REPLY MAIL
FIRST-CLASS MAIL   PERMIT NO. 75738   LOS ANGELES CA

POSTAGE WILL BE PAID BY ADDRESSEE

GOLDEN AGE BOOK CLUB
GALAXY PRESS
7051 HOLLYWOOD BLVD
LOS ANGELES CA 90028-9771

Clamorously, now, he cried, "James! You have mistaken the direction! The coast is to the *east*! James!"

"I haven't mistaken anything," said Mitchell.

"But . . . but . . . good gracious, this is the direction all those troops took! We're going into the very heart of the battle area! I *demand* that you turn around."

"Demand away," said Mitchell. "If you don't like this direction, you can get out."

"No. Oh, no. My goodness. I can't stay in Yin-Meng! Please, my boy, have you no sense of duty to your father? Have you no sense of duty?"

"Father," said Mitchell, "we're headed for Shunkien. If you would rather come with us than stay behind, settle down and ride."

"Shunkien," wept the reverend. "But, my boy, it's in a state of *siege*. You can never even approach the city!"

"I got orders to deliver a box and a keg to Shunkien, siege or no siege. And whether you like it or not, that's our destination. Now put up or shut up."

The reverend subsided for a long while and then he muttered, "You always were a wayward boy, James. A Marine and then a chorus girl and now you defy your own father."

Rolling deeper into hostile China, the reverend wiped the emotional mist from his glasses and watched the rough miles go by.

Chapter Ten

AT the end of a rough twenty-five miles, during which they had been lucky enough to receive no attention from occasional cavalry squadrons, the sergeant gave up the wheel to Toughey.

Yawning and rubbing his eyes, Toughey slid under. Mitchell paused as he started to get into the rear seat.

"This is noon, Thursday," said Mitchell. "Or is it?"

"I think so," said Toughey, yawning cavernously.

"We ought to be rolling in there before night—if we can get through the Japanese lines ahead. Don't drive too fast."

"Okay, Sarge. You'll be as safe as a babe in a cradle. Cork off to your heart's desire."

Mitchell got into the rear seat beside the sleeping girl and Toughey started up.

The sergeant looked at his pack lying in the bottom of the car. He pulled it to him and fumbled with the buckles, searching for an extra package of cigarettes. His hand encountered the cold side of the whisky bottle.

He glanced sideways at the girl and then at the back of the reverend's neck. The reverend was sleeping, pince-nez awry, mouth open to display gold teeth. Toughey was intent on his driving.

It wouldn't hurt, thought Mitchell. Not one small swig.

71

He was getting so jittery he could hardly sit still. He pulled the bottle out of the pack and read the label:

Canadian Whisky. Five Years Old. One Quart.

He broke the seal and touched the cork.

Somehow he would have to bluff his way through the Japanese lines around Shunkien. His lack of orders would make it hard. What would he tell them?

He began to struggle with the cork. He needed a drink to steady him down. Just one and then he'd quit.

Again he looked at the reverend's nodding pate. He frowned a little. He was so tired he couldn't sleep and everything was passing in review behind his eyes. It seemed only that morning that he had slid through the mission gates to head for the coast and the States. He had been wearing a denim shirt and jeans, the kind his father sometimes gave to his workmen. He had some biscuits in his pocket and the contents of the poor box—which was not much.

He remembered how that money had scorched his thigh, how certain he had been that Jehovah would open up the heavens and knock him flat with a thunderbolt. Mile after mile he had watched the heavens and when nothing had happened he began to suspect that a later doom was waiting for him.

But he had needed that money. It had bought him meals and places to sleep, little as it was.

Since that time he had never passed a church without recalling that theft.

Things were different now. For fifteen years he had lived on gunpowder and excitement and flaming drink. The fifteen years before that had been spent in those mission walls behind them, praying every night, reading the Bible every day, saying grace lengthily before each meal, attending church and listening to his father's droning sermons six hours out of every Sunday.

He had not been allowed to play with his Chinese friends because a white boy, according to his father, had a part to share in the "white man's burden."

What a funny kid he must have been! Crammed with biblical texts, living in fear of great and awful catastrophe when he had done wrong, holding his father in awe because the Chinese all about knew his gift of doctoring and considered him a great man.

He recalled the hour when he knew he could not bear it longer. He was alone in his room staring at a chromo of the manger scene upon the wall. He had slipped into the village the night before to talk with friends. It had been against the law and he had been detected. In his ears still rang the Voice of Doom which had intoned his wickedness. He was wayward. He would not conform. Unless he mended his ways, his was the Path to Eternal Darkness. His supper had been withheld and rebellion born of hunger had sent him forth.

He was Condemned Forever. He could do no more wrong. And he had robbed the poor box on his way through the gates.

That was fifteen years ago and there, on the front seat, was his kidnaped father, sleeping with his mouth open, with his collar unfastened and sticking out under his ear, with his coat in rags and his pants leg slit. . . .

A droning sound was in the air and Mitchell, sensing

73

rather than hearing it, glanced down the road behind them, expecting to see another car. The road was empty fore and aft.

In sudden consternation, Mitchell slid the bottle hastily into his pack and leaned outside into the stream of wind.

Above and behind them, about a thousand feet high, roared three Japanese Kawasaki KDA-5s.

They were spread out, one behind the other in dive formation, and Mitchell was looking at them head-on as they started down.

"Toughey!" yelled Mitchell. "STOP!"

Toughey tromped upon the screaming brakes and the car slewed sideways in billowing dust, Toughey fighting the wheel.

"GET OUT!" shouted Mitchell, snatching at the girl's arm and dragging her with him. They plunged over the door, the girl still half-asleep, hitting the road before the car had stopped moving.

The reverend's glasses flew from his nose as his inertia threw him ahead. Toughey had him by the coat.

A chattering blast filled the air, audible above the shriek of wires and yammer of engines. Vicious spurts of dust streaked along the road toward the car.

Mitchell threw the girl into the protection of a ditch and jumped up again. Toughey was almost out of the car, dragging the reverend with him.

A small, hurtling shadow flashed across the earth at Mitchell's feet. He cried, "DOWN!" and threw himself flat on his face. An explosion battered the air over him. Dust geysered high, fragments hung for an instant against the sun, turned and dropped lazily down in a wide circle, pattering like hail.

Three shadows in quick succession spread their wings over Mitchell and then were gone. His ears began to roar in the descending silence. The three planes had gone.

Mitchell got up, spitting bits of highway from his mouth. His right side felt numb and damp but he had no thought for it in that instant.

The car was spewing smoke from under its punctured hood. The reverend was standing stupidly on the running board looking down and saying, "Dear me, dear me," over and over in a toneless voice.

Toughey was trying to sit up, his big face gnarled with pain, recovering from shock. He looked down at his torn canvas legging and his ripped green pants and swore through clenched teeth.

Mitchell was instantly at his side. "Hit bad?"

"M'leg. Those —— —— —— —— ——!"

"Dear me," said the reverend.

"Shut up," snapped Mitchell, glaring at his father. "Dig out my pack and be quick about it."

The reverend stood where he was, staring down at the pool of blood which began to grow about Toughey's foot.

Goldy came up out of the ditch, a dazed expression on her smudged face. Now that she was wholly awake, it seemed to her that time had telescoped the group before her into the walled mission yard. She saw Toughey stretched out and Mitchell's command penetrated to her.

Swiftly she hauled Mitchell's pack into the road. He pulled it closer without looking up and fumbled for his brown first-aid packet.

"You hurt bad?" she whispered to Toughey.

"Naw," he growled between pain-clenched teeth. "You . . . you can't kill a Marine."

Mitchell had Toughey's bayonet and was slitting the legging. He cut the laces of the shoe and pulled it off.

Goldy swallowed hard and knelt beside Toughey. The reverend started to get down beside Mitchell but the sergeant thrust him away.

The bone was broken above the ankle in a compound fracture and Mitchell looked at it with hopeless eyes. He pulled the ring of the first-aid packet and then seemed to remember something.

"Lemme see," begged Toughey.

Goldy held him down. "No. It's not as bad as it looks. You'll be all right, big boy."

"Father," said Mitchell in a hard voice. "You used to be good at this sort of thing. Patch him up."

The reverend knelt down and took the bandages. Mitchell poured water out of his canteen into the dixie and looked around. Gasoline was leaking from the tank and he saturated the cushion stuffings with it. Over the green blaze he boiled the water.

Toughey's face was the color of limestone. Mitchell reached into his pack and pulled out the Canadian whisky. Nobody noticed its presence or remarked it when he forced the amber fluid down Toughey's throat.

The reverend set the bone and splinted it with bayonet and scabbard. Mitchell gave Toughey another drink and then put the bottle back into his pack.

"Sarge," said Toughey, sitting up. "I . . . I can't walk with this thing. You and Goldy and the reverend—"

"Shut up," said Mitchell angrily.

"But I can't . . ."

"You'll walk," said Mitchell.

Toughey looked at him with contracted brows. "But I'll slow you down. I think—"

"Never mind thinking. I'll do the thinking around here. Get up!"

Toughey tried and Goldy looked on, horrified.

"Get up!" snapped Mitchell.

"Ain't you got any heart?" cried Goldy. "Good God, if he tried to walk on that—"

"Pipe down," said Mitchell. He put his arm around Toughey and pulled him erect. Toughey leaned heavily against him.

Mitchell motioned toward the car. "Get his rifle and pack, Goldy. And get into them."

"Huh?"

"You heard me. Father, do you see that keg?"

"Ah . . . yes. Yes, yes. Of course I see it, James."

"Well, pick it up and put it on your shoulder and find out how much it weighs."

"But, my boy!"

"Pick it up!"

The reverend polished his glasses in grief and then looked at his son's unrelenting face. He sighed and started to haul the keg out of the car but when he felt its weight he paused, about to draw himself up in loud protest. He caught another glimpse of the gunnery sergeant's face. The reverend boosted the keg to his shoulder with a despairing grunt.

"Somewhere ahead," said Mitchell, "we'll run into the Japanese lines. Maybe something can be done. We're about twenty miles from Shunkien."

"Practically there," mourned Goldy, feeling for the first time in her life just how heavy a pack and rifle can be.

"March," said Mitchell and moved off, more than half carrying the huge Toughey.

Chapter Eleven

TWO flares burned in the darkness and by their jumpy light could be seen the irregular pattern of sandbags stretched across the road and topped with barbed wire. Silhouetted in the foreground was a triangular stack of rifles and gleaming to one side squatted a spraddle-legged machine gun, manned by a sleepy Japanese crew.

A short row of tents faced the road, glowing with inner light and patterned with grotesque shadows, caricatures of the officers within.

A stocky sentry snapped erect to the right of the machine gunners. Rifle at port, he advanced two cautious paces, staring into the darkness down the road.

Four shadows were less dark than the night beyond.

"Todomeru!" barked the sentry. "Halt!"

The machine gunners popped up like jack-in-the-boxes. The shadows stopped moving on the walls of the tent and then surged toward the entrances.

Staggering under the almost inert weight of Toughey, Mitchell advanced until he could be seen in the light of the flares. Behind him the reverend stopped, panting, to set down the keg. Goldy paused uncertainly.

Mitchell saw an ammunition box on his right. He eased

Toughey down to it and then stood erect again. He felt curiously lightheaded and his side was aching. He had not dared explore the wound.

Several curious officers closed into a semicircle about him. Two sentries moved warily down to better watch the other members of the party.

The silence was very long. Behind the impassive faces of the officers, astonishment was rife. There was no mistaking the globe and anchor and eagle on this haggard soldier's cap. Officers of the Mikado were not prepared to see a United States Marine.

Mitchell started to speak in Shantung dialect and then stopped. It made no impression upon them. He swung back to English.

"I am Gunnery Sergeant James Mitchell of the United States Marines. I am under orders to proceed to Shunkien and report to United States Consul Jackson of that city. You will please let me pass."

The officers stood where they were, just as blank as ever. Irritably, Mitchell started to speak again but a small, pigeon-breasted fellow, with a face as round and shining as the reverend's bald head, stepped a pace forward.

"I speak English. Why do you want to go to Shunkien?"

"I am under orders from the commanding officer of the United States cruiser *Miami*. I wish to pass through your lines with my . . . my landing force."

The Japanese massaged his face very thoughtfully, much like a sleek cat adjusting its whiskers. He stepped back and conversed very rapidly with a quick-eyed gentleman of higher rank.

Presently he spoke again. "Why do you wish to go to Shunkien? Did you not know that the city is under siege?"

"I am under orders," said Mitchell stubbornly.

"It is impossible. We are very sorry. You, of course, have your orders with you?"

"The first Japanese PC I ran into relieved me of them."

"Hmmmmm. This is very irregular. Have you a receipt for those orders?"

Mitchell stilled his wrath. He reached into his right blouse pocket and found the spot spongy. The piece of paper he brought forth was stained a sticky red. He passed it over.

The Japanese clustered around their English-speaking member. They moved en masse to the front of a tent and inclined the slip to the light. They looked at each other and shook their heads.

The linguist stepped back to Mitchell, chest thrust forward importantly. "This might very well be anything. There is nothing but part of a signature here. I am sorry, but we cannot accept this. It is necessary that you be detained pending further investigation."

Mitchell tried to muster up the energy to sound off long and loud. But he was too weary and too angry to say a great deal. It was, perhaps, fortunate.

"I am under orders to proceed to Shunkien and I am to be there before Saturday. It is imperative that you allow me to pass. If you do not—"

"Enough of this," said the Japanese. "You will only be detained long enough for us to confirm these orders. Have we any proof that you are what you say you are? Perhaps you are renegades masquerading. Perhaps you have deserted. Ah . . . What do you have in that keg?"

"I do not know. I am under orders—"

"Yes, of course. You have said that before." The Japanese turned and spoke swiftly to his commanding officer who, in turn, rattled orders to the sentries.

The soldiers thrust the reverend off the keg and rolled it forward. More commands were passed and a broadsword was produced.

When Mitchell lunged ahead, his way was barred by bayonets crossed before him. He stopped and looked helplessly and angrily on.

The keg was broken open and tipped on its side. A flood of golden guineas slid into the dust.

The Japanese officers clicked their tongues and felt of the coins and looked askance at Mitchell.

"This is very bad," said the linguist. "You may have looted this somewhere. We shall check up."

"How long will that take?" said Mitchell bitterly.

"Two days. Three days. A week." He shrugged.

Another Japanese officer marched up with a file of infantry and indicated to Mitchell that his group was to fall in. Toughey did not respond to a thump on the back and a Japanese soldier, before Mitchell could stop him, yanked Toughey to his feet.

Mitchell struck and the soldier went down.

Toughey lay in the road, unconscious, until a stretcher was produced and he was loaded aboard.

Three men were detailed to Mitchell personally and the bayonets glittered brightly in the flares. Wearily he allowed himself to be shoved along. He knew he had not helped his case.

Two days. Three days. A week?

Chapter Twelve

M ITCHELL, James, gunnery sergeant USMC, was
stretched on a cot, alone in a small tent. The Japanese
had ample facilities for housing strange prisoners, as only a fool
would bother to feed a captured Chinese soldier and several
officers had gone down in the din of battle to the eternal glory
of Nippon. But Mitchell, James, gunnery sergeant USMC,
was not appreciative of the fact.

He had swabbed iodine into his wounded side and had
padded the place as well as he could, but it felt as feverish as
his brow. Images danced a little and he had to concentrate
to keep them in their place.

The bottle of whisky was standing on his pack at attention.
The contents were lowered exactly to the place where Toughey
had put them and no farther.

Mitchell was reading the label over and over, but it didn't
say *Canadian Whisky. Five Years Old. One Quart,* anymore.
He didn't know what it said but he was reading the label
anyway.

Sometimes he thought he could read a line from the Old
Testament across the white face. He had had that hallucination
before. In Gothic type, across that label, was scrawled *Give
strong drink unto him that is ready to perish, and wine unto those
that be of heavy hearts. Prov. 31:6.*

Puzzled he read the invisible over and over again and it became more and more clear to him. He clenched his eyes in heavy thought and opened them again to read anew the Gothic type which had danced there for fifteen years.

He looked toward the closed flap of the tent as though his vision could bridge twelve miles and penetrate the walls of Shunkien.

This was Friday and night was coming on. He could see the hard, walnut visage of Captain Davis coming out of the canvas wall to silently look at him. He blinked the phantom away and slowly returned his attention to the fantastic label.

Give strong drink unto him that is ready to perish . . .

Why did the label read that way? Why had it read that way for fifteen years?

His throat was dry and hot and the incessant clatter of a far-off gun hurt his head. He raised up on one elbow and read the label again.

Give strong drink . . .

In the next tent Goldy sat on an empty case and watched Toughey's chest rise and fall beneath a mustard-colored blanket. His broken nose made him snuffle as he breathed. He was lying half awake as though coming back from a trip to another world. He turned his head and looked at Goldy for a long time.

"Hello," said Toughey.

"How are you doin'?"

"Okay. Get caught up on your sleep?"

"Yeah. I thought I could sleep for a year but at the end of

fourteen hours I couldn't lie still another minute. How long do you think we'll be here?"

"Duration of the war for all I know. You seen the sarge?"

"I looked into his tent a little while ago. These Japanese let you roam around as long as you stay peaceful."

"What'd he say?"

"He didn't even know I was there. He's layin' on his back looking at a whisky bottle he's got propped up on his pack."

"Holy hell!" cried Toughey, trying desperately to sit up and failing to make it unassisted. "Good God, Goldy, if you know what's good for us, grab that bottle quick! Where'd he get it?"

"He had it all the time so far as I know. I just remembered that he gave you a couple snorts when that lead bouquet got wrapped around you."

"That's so!" said Toughey. "I was so far gone I never clicked. Listen, Goldy. Shove off and grab that bottle and bust it. We'll never get out of here if he gets himself three sheets to the wind. You don't know that guy. He'd tear up this whole Japanese outfit to get another snort once he got started."

"He looked pretty peaceful to me," said Goldy, not moving. "Besides, what's the use? We'll be shipped back to the coast and he'll have plenty of time to recover. As for me, I'd just as soon we did get shipped back."

"He's got his orders," said Toughey. "And if he can't carry on, it's his finish!"

"Don't get all worked up, pal," said Goldy. "You hear that

shootin'? Well, that's the end of Shunkien according to our cat-faced friend."

"That don't make no difference. If the Scandinavians took the town, we still got our orders. Hey, what you know about me carryin' that gold all over the place!"

Goldy laughed at him.

Toughey's single-track brain reverted to Mitchell. "You better go get that bottle if you ever expect to get under weigh from this dump. I've served with the sarge for six years and I know what makes him tick. Sober, he's the best Marine in the outfit but drunk, he's the damnedest, most scatterbrained sap you ever met. And he's the only one who can talk us out of this mess."

Goldy sat on the case without any signs of moving off and Toughey sank back, giving up.

The reverend came into the tent shortly after, looking very downcast. He stood gazing at Toughey as though about to read his funeral service and then removed his glasses and shined them up and replaced them.

"It's terrible. Terrible!" said the reverend.

"What?" said Goldy.

"I've seen two of my trucks! I shall write to the State Department about this!"

"Probably," said Goldy.

"Undoubtedly," wept the reverend. "They were stolen by Chinese and now the Japanese have them, and though I fail to understand how this came about, it is certain that I shall make every effort to collect indemnity from the Japanese army." He gave way under the strength of his emotion and polished his glasses again. When he had carefully replaced them and had stroked their long black ribbon out straight, he continued. "I shall call the attention of the State Department to this in the strongest terms."

"I'm callin' your attention," said Goldy, "to Toughey's leg—in terms strong enough to scorch your ears. You haven't looked at it all day."

"Aw, I'm all right," said Toughey.

The reverend was about to take Toughey's word for it when he caught the full force of Goldy's glare. Hastily he pulled up the blanket and inspected Toughey's leg for possible infection which he did not find.

"It seems to be mending nicely," said the reverend. "That is," he added recalling professional prudence, "there is no evidence that it is *not* mending."

"Did you set it straight?" said Goldy.

"Oh, yes. It is a very simple fracture and would not have compounded without the shrapnel wound. The break is confined to the tibia, leaving the femur untouched. The extensor tendon is unaffected and the internal malleolus is intact. The astragalus is bruised slightly but seems to have been spared harm by the shoe. Thus I doubt that the articulation will be hampered upon healing."

"It's all Greek to me," said Goldy.

"I beg your pardon," replied the reverend. "But most medical terms are derived from Latin."

"Is that so," said Goldy without any great interest. "I get it that you're puttin' us wise to the fact that he'll be toesmithing with the best of 'em."

"Eh?" said the reverend.

She looked at him in surprise and then decided to let it pass.

"I have just heard," said the reverend, "that Shunkien's walls have been taken. I have also employed my time in trying to convince the Japanese colonel that he is doing us a grave injustice by refusing to allow us to return to the coast. I might say that I brought the strongest pressure to bear but he seemed impatient."

"You better talk to the sarge before you go hangin' out the wash to the Japanese."

"But I thought if I personally could be allowed—"

"So you're tryin' to shin the chains," said Toughey with bitterness. "You better get wise to yourself. The sarge is in command around here and you better talk to him. If he says you can slip cable and full-speed out of here, okay. As long as you got into this outfit, he's responsible for you."

"You mean James?" gaped the reverend.

"I mean Gunnery Sergeant Mitchell," said Toughey hoarsely.

"You mean I am to get his permission to leave? Even if the Japanese say that I can?"

"I mean just that," said Toughey with a regulation growl. "And I ain't got no delusions about him lettin' you go. What if the skipper found out we was the cause of castin' you adrift in this country and maybe lettin' you get bumped off? There'd be hell to pay. If the sarge knew you was plannin' to run out on him, you'd think a buzz saw was somethin' to eat for indigestion."

The reverend removed his glasses and scrubbed off the fog. "To think he would place his own father in such a predicament! But I did my best. I tried to raise him to be a credit to his church. And these are the thanks I get. These are the thanks! He exposes me to imprisonment, perhaps death. . . ."

"I bet you raised him," said Goldy with heavy sarcasm.

"To the best of my ability," wept the reverend. "I tried to place his feet upon the godly path and the only appreciation he ever gave me was to run away. He even . . ." and here he almost broke down. "He even robbed the poor box when he left."

"Robbed the poor box?" said Goldy. "How much was in it?"

"Three dollars at the very least. It required months to recover from the shock of knowing that my boy was not only disobedient but also a thief. God is my witness that I strove to teach him the way to salvation and now I find that he runs about the country with a . . ." He caught himself in time on that one and hastily plunged on.

"I find that he is a Marine, a drunkard, capable of placing his own father in a perilous position, of stealing a car . . ."

Goldy's eyes were intent upon him. "So you fed him full of hellfire and damnation, did you? And he couldn't stand it any longer and took a powder. And he's been running ever since."

"What?" said the reverend.

"Skip it," said Goldy. "You got the least to cry about and you're the only one that's turnin' on the rain." She got up and looked down at Toughey. "Want anything before I go?"

91

"Yeah. F'gawd's sake get that . . . you know . . . away from him. We're in this deep enough now without that."

Goldy went out, her hands thrust deeply into the pockets of her swagger coat, her platinum hair escaping from beneath the cap with the jockey brim.

A sentry came alertly to attention as she emerged and watched her closely as she moved down the line to Mitchell's tent. She whistled a bar of jazz with elaborate carelessness and when she looked through the flap of Mitchell's tent, the bottle had vanished.

"How's the feet?" said Mitchell, sitting up and swinging his legs down.

"Okay," said Goldy. "Of course, they have been in better shape. Any news yet?"

"Not yet," said Mitchell wearily. "This is a hell of a note. We're twelve miles from Shunkien and we can't get a yard closer. Listen to that row out there. The little boys in mustard must be moppin' the place up. But that won't change my orders. I got to get there!"

"Sure," said Goldy, soothingly.

"I suppose you won't care one way or the other," said Mitchell. "Maybe you'd rather steer for the coast."

"Maybe. It's a cinch I ain't got any billing in Shunkien. Don't take it so hard, Sarge. You tried. . . ."

"I haven't stopped trying," he replied sharply. "By God, they won't dare keep that keg and turn us back. We've come this far and we'll go the whole way. I been thinking it might be a good bet to grab a rifle off one of these sentries. . . . But I know I'm crazy."

She sat down on the foot of his cot. "Don't pull anything like that."

"Aw, I know I can't. But I'm going crazy sitting here twiddling my thumbs. I guess you're pretty sore at me for getting you into this."

"I've been madder in my life," said Goldy.

He grinned in sudden appreciation of the gallantry of her and turned a little to face her.

She got up abruptly, backing toward the flap.

"I didn't mean anything," said Mitchell. "You act like I was poison."

"Good night," said Goldy, backing out. "Sweet dreams."

She was gone and Mitchell watched the flap stop swaying. He lay back on his cot, staring at the sloping canvas above him.

The angry rumble of the attack beat against him in waves. It matched the storm of his own spirits and made him more restless than ever. But sleep came to him at last.

Toward midnight the ferocity of the mopping-up diminished and Mitchell began to wake up, sensible of the change even in his slumber.

He put on his cap and buttoned up his blouse. He went to the flap of his tent and looked out across the active camp. Troops were coming up from the west, fagged after a forced march, ready to fill the gaps in the ranks so that the Japanese could circle out and cut off all retreat from Shunkien.

Mitchell's appearance conjured a sentry out of the shadows. Slowly Mitchell began to stroll down the company street toward the headquarters tents with the sentry pacing alertly at his heels.

All was activity despite the lateness of the hour. Every officer was dressed and furiously busy. A stream of runners came and went from the largest of the tents.

Mitchell waited for half an hour, ignored by all, before he caught sight of the cocky linguist. He stopped him by stepping in his road.

"Is there any word yet?" said Mitchell.

It took a moment for the officer to shift the gears of his mind. Impatiently then, anxious to be gone on his business, he said, "Certainly. It came hours ago."

"Good news?" said Mitchell, eagerly. "I can proceed into Shunkien?"

"See me about it later."

Mitchell was still in his path and the officer tried to dodge around him and found Mitchell still blocking the way.

"I got orders to be in Shunkien by tomorrow morning," said Mitchell doggedly. "If you have word from the east I want to know what it is."

The Japanese was about to bite off another short answer when he recalled the import of the news. It was worse than a mere verbal rebuff.

"Your orders are on file with the second division but our colonel refuses to allow you to proceed toward Shunkien. Your burden is to be returned to you and you are to be started for the coast tomorrow morning. We cannot allow you either an armed escort or any vehicle. Now get out of my way."

"You refuse to let me through to the city?" persisted Mitchell.

"Naturally. We have too much to do already without being bothered with you. Those are the orders of our colonel and if you attempt to disobey them we can only resort to imprisonment of you and your party for the duration of this unfortunate incident. Thank you very much and get out of my way."

The officer ducked around him and was gone. Mitchell stared after him with mayhem plain upon his face. The sentry, alarmed, prodded Mitchell in the back and motioned toward Mitchell's tent.

Dispiritedly, Mitchell trooped back down the company street to throw himself on his cot and beat his clenched fist into his pillow. He knew his fate was written. There were too many Japanese swarming between this camp and Shunkien. Any attempt at force would be suicidal.

He knew these things and he also knew his orders.

But he could do nothing. He had failed.

He lay back, wincing as he touched his aching side, and stared holes into the darkness.

Chapter Thirteen

BILLOWING smoke from the burning shores of the Huangpu rolled in suffocating waves across the decks of the USS *Miami.* Saturday's sun made small impression on the gloom which overhung Shanghai and now it sat straight overhead, a spinning sphere as red as blood.

Blackstone, V. G., commanding, was piped over the side. He was in a mood as lowering as the day. Unhappy Captain Davis started to retreat from the gangway but he had been observed.

"Davis!" said Blackstone. "Report to my quarters immediately."

Davis followed with none of the esprit he had displayed in a score of landing parties and in a dozen battles.

Blackstone hurled his cap to his desk and sat down so hard that his chair shrieked in protest. His big red hands shuffled through his papers and came up with a radio.

Davis stood just inside the door, cap in hand, feeling much as he had the time a live grenade of the tin can variety had fallen in his foxhole in Nic.

Blackstone read the radio and balled it up. He spun around and glared. "I suppose you think the C-in-C invited me over for a tea party. I suppose you think he complimented me upon my strategy." Unnecessarily, he roared, "Well, he didn't!

I've been on a carpet hotter'n boilerplates. And all because I was fool enough to listen to a half-baked captain of Marines! You see this?" He rattled the radiogram in the air and then crunched it up again. "They haven't heard of your damned Marines in Shunkien. Jackson is yowling for relief and here we are reporting back in Shanghai without having completed our mission. Here it is noon Saturday!"

"They've got until midnight," said Davis feebly, his usually walnut visage a dull red.

"Bah! I'll tell you what's happened to them. That booze-fighting sergeant of yours got himself scuppered with liquor and he's somewhere in Shantung right now spending that keg of gold!"

"Sir," said Davis, stiffly, "Mitchell—"

"To hell with Mitchell! Two Americans in the consulate are already down with cholera and it's only a matter of hours before they all die! They'll all be dead! And who'll take the blasting for that? Me! Ohhhhhhh," he shivered, "if I could only get my hands on that precious pair, I'd—"

"Perhaps they've been killed, sir," said Captain Davis.

"Killed! They better get themselves killed before they ever show up on this ship again! I should have known better than to let myself be talked into this. 'He knows the country!' 'He's a good man.' 'He won't get into trouble!' *Awrrrrrrr!* They've had time to walk to Timbuktu and back."

"I still think, sir," said Davis without any hope whatever, "that they'll report. It must have been pretty difficult getting through. You said yourself that they might encounter difficulties. That they might even be killed. You said—"

"So you throw my own words back in my teeth, do you? See here, Captain Davis, I'll have you know that I'm running this ship. No cockeyed Marine is going to stand there and tell *me* what I said. You've said too much already. Ohhhhhhh, this will go pretty hard with you. Now get out. I'm sick of looking at you."

Davis hurriedly removed himself and stomped down the passageway back into wardroom country, swearing as he went. He stopped once and glared at empty space.

"So you can't follow orders, eh? So you go stumbling around China getting ginned up, do you? By God, I'll bobtail you to a sailor! I'll cut off your stripes and make you eat them. I'll get you a bad conduct and send you to Portsmouth and string you up to the yard. *Awrrrrr!* Make a fool out of me, will you?!"

A mess attendant came out and stared wide-eyed at the empty space and then at the captain.

Davis turned and almost ran over the boy.

The mess attendant vanished, shaking at the expression he had seen on the captain's face, wondering that he had escaped with his life.

Chapter Fourteen

IT was not until one o'clock Saturday that Mitchell, James, gunnery sergeant USMC, was finally convinced by the Japanese that the Shunkien area was not to be crossed. At least, he appeared to be convinced, as he gave up.

A wind was blowing down from the northern plains, digging up big clouds of yellow dust. It stirred in the skirts of the olive green overcoat and lifted and lowered its left lapel. Mitchell's cheeks were sunken and his eyes burned too brightly. He stood very straight before three Japanese officers.

"Thanks to an error of your planes," said Mitchell, "it will be necessary for me to request a stretcher in which to transport my command. And I also wish to count the gold in that keg before I accept it from you."

"You think, perhaps, that we are dishonest?" said the proud officer snappishly.

"If there's any of it gone, I'll be checked for it the rest of my life. You will have enough to answer when my commanding officer knows I have been detained."

It was sheer bluff, but this same bluff was giving him freedom at least.

"We care nothing about your commanding officer. In fact," stated the Japanese officer gratingly, "we have something to say ourselves about the impudence of the United States sending armed Marines into our battle areas. If you wish to know the truth, it is very likely that we shall report this in the strongest terms. We object to such a clumsy attempt at gathering military intelligence about our fighting tactics."

"So that's why you won't let me go on."

"Do you think we are stubborn without reason? Do you think we wish to have our activities against Shunkien, our methods of attack, our losses, our armament, our numerical strength, reported? You swaggering, blustering, overbearing whites think to have something to say about this campaign. I regret our ability to furnish them with such intelligence. You will find that news of you will have gone ahead and you are to report into every Japanese post of command between here and Liaochow. Failure at any one post will cost you your liberty. We regret," he added with great insincerity, "our inability to provide you with conveyance and escort. But we have other things to do besides shepherd lost soldiers."

"That's all right about that," said Mitchell with strange docility. "Give me a stretcher and we'll get out of here."

The Japanese officer turned to his major and received his concurrence. The stretcher was brought up.

Mitchell turned to the reverend. "Take the other end of this and we'll get Toughey."

"But . . . but he must weigh—"

"Never mind what he weighs. Snap into it."

The reverend sighed, deploring his son's tone of voice. He took the front end of the stretcher and marched.

Toughey looked for news in Mitchell's face. "Is it east or west, Sarge?"

"East."

Toughey's face lengthened but he said nothing. Goldy was standing at the back of his tent. She gave Mitchell a quick glance.

"We walk?" said Goldy.

"Naw," said Toughey. "The general is goin' to give us his private car and send half his army along as escort."

They carefully placed Toughey on the stretcher and Mitchell cut his objections short.

They all felt the strange intensity in Mitchell. His hands were trembling and he was holding himself too straight.

The reverend staggered under the weight of his end.

"March," said Mitchell.

The reverend marched, staggering as though under the effect of all the drinks he had never drunk. His half of Toughey weighed a hundred and eight pounds.

They set Toughey down before the officers' tents. The keg was there and Mitchell tipped it over.

Mitchell divided the heaped coins three ways and indicated that Goldy and the reverend were to get down and count.

They counted and the reverend's mutter of "hundred and seven, hundred and eight, hundred and nine . . ." was a great handicap to both the sergeant and the girl.

Mitchell's fingers were practiced and to him these sovereigns were so many chips. He set them up in piles of twenty-five until he was barricaded by gold. He scooped some of the other two piles into his reach and checked them.

The Japanese officers looked on with great indignation but Mitchell calmly went on counting.

103

They finished at last and took their tallies. The gold was all there. Mitchell dumped it back into the keg, shook it down and battened the lid. He asked for a section of rope and got it. With this he lashed the keg between the handles of his end of the stretcher.

"You goin' to lug that thing clear to the coast?" said Goldy. "I don't even think you can lift it!"

"Father is going to carry my pack," said Mitchell shrugging out of it.

"I . . . er . . . what? Good gracious, James, have you no feeling? Even that short distance almost pulled my arms from their sockets. I . . ."

Mitchell was fixing the pack so that the reverend could wear it. His father looked on, taking his pince-nez on and off distractedly. But when the pack was offered he resignedly let it be put upon him. It almost tipped him over backwards and his glasses fogged alarmingly.

Standing very straight again, Mitchell faced the linguist. "You were forced to send a communication relative to my orders. Each Japanese PC will try to do this and my progress will be greatly delayed. You can save your brother officers much time by giving me a pass which will recognize me to them as well as to any roving patrols of your cavalry."

Goldy looked at him perplexedly. He was so very straight, so very precise. She had seen a man look like that once, just before he had fallen on his face in a dead faint. But were the rules applying to adagio dancers applicable to Marines?

The Japanese talked it over gravely. The sound of marching

feet was in the air and they glanced down the road toward an approaching company of reinforcements.

The major gestured abruptly and moved off to greet the new outfit's commander. The other officer followed him, leaving the impatient linguist alone.

This officer entered the headquarters tent and came out a moment later, bearing a printed card on the bottom of which a string of ideographs were not yet dry.

Contemptuously he thrust it in Mitchell's direction but before Mitchell's fingers touched it, the Japanese dropped it to the road and walked off.

Mitchell stood for a moment looking at the officer's stiff back and then stooped for the pass. He blew on the ink until it was dry and placed it in his pocket.

"March," said Mitchell, taking up his end of the leaden stretcher.

The reverend took two or three steps to the left and right as though his feet wanted to get out from under. Goldy looked critically at his dancing form and found it bad. She had gotten used to the weight of Toughey's pack and rifle, had found how to lean forward to steady the weight. But then, Goldy's career made her more adaptable where balance was concerned than the reverend's.

They moved on down the road, walking in the ditch to get by the seemingly endless line of Japanese troops which had halted to await further orders. Mitchell did not glance at the curious barrage of eyes. He was looking straight ahead as though he could see all the way to infinity through the yellow day. The wind felt good against his hot cheeks except when a rack of shivers took him.

The four were silent as they trudged. The reverend eagerly kept his ears cocked, certain that James would stop to rest every tenth step.

But James kept right on shoving the stretcher into the reverend and the reverend could do nothing but keep going. Soon he had resigned himself to the numbness which crept up from his wrists to his shoulders, down his shoulders to the small of his back. His legs appeared to be manufactured of rubber and his glasses, for want of wiping, grew so foggy he could hardly see where he went. James took care of that.

The Japanese camp diminished behind them, to finally vanish. And then the endless plains were on every side, relieved only where the wrecked and deserted railroad's poles cut sharply against the sky.

"Halt," said Mitchell.

The reverend set down the end of the stretcher with a weary thump and shucked out of the pack which had chewed at least a foot into each shoulder. He sat down disconsolately and wiped his glasses, his movements very slow.

"Feel all right?" said Goldy to Toughey.

"I feel like hell," said Toughey. "When I think what the skipper is going to do to us when we show up without having followed orders . . ." He shuddered.

Mitchell brought out the pass and put it in his father's hands. "Can you read any of this?"

"No. That's Japanese."

"Sure it's Japanese," said Goldy. "Did you think them guys back there talked Eskimo?"

Mitchell took the paper back and looked holes into it. He turned it around in his hands, muttering, "If I could only be sure. . . ."

"You got an idea?" cried Toughey, struggling up on his elbows. And when Mitchell did not answer, Toughey turned to Goldy. "He's got one all right. He always looks like he's chewin' somethin' when he gets it hot. He's got one!"

Mitchell was still staring at his paper, his jaws pulsing, his teeth clenched.

"Cut the suspense," said Goldy. "Are we goin' to walk to the coast or have you thought up how to steal an airplane or something?"

Mitchell looked down at Toughey. "We're going to Shunkien."

"Oh, good gracious," mourned the reverend. "If we get caught, and I'm certain we will be, they'll lock us up for months! Have you no feeling, James? Really, I should rather carry this stretcher all the way to Liaochow than to be a prisoner for the remainder of my life. James, have you no heart?"

"Shut up," said Toughey. "Orders is orders."

"It's shorter," said Goldy, already aware of the blisters she had lately contracted. "But how you going to pull this off, huh? They didn't listen to you back there, why should they listen to you someplace else?"

"Only posts in the rear have been told about us," said Mitchell, thinking aloud. "Posts to the south of Shunkien

107

won't know a thing. And if this pass merely says to let a sergeant and party through the Japanese lines, they'll honor it anywhere."

"But if we don't report . . ." began the reverend.

"A United States Consulate is the same as USA soil," said Mitchell. "To hell with what happens once we're there."

"I beg pardon, James?"

"I said to hell with it."

"We'll be caught," said the reverend. "James, have you no—"

"No! Pick up that pack."

The reverend picked it up and struggled into it. His dance as he got the stretcher up was more prolonged than before.

They headed south.

"I *knew* he had an idea," crowed Toughey.

"It's shorter anyhow," said Goldy.

And after that they slogged in silence with the wind pushing them and stirring the rags of the reverend's coattails.

Chapter Fifteen

THE Japanese had entered, purged and executed Shunkien. Patrols marched through the streets, turning aside to blast out lurking Chinese troops, occasionally running into a sniper's bullets, singling out a few civilian examples to put the remains of the city upon its good behavior.

The south gate of the town was shut. Machine guns pointed both outward and inward as a double precaution; sentries stood stiff and alert. Weary soldiers sat in groups, staring at the ground in complete exhaustion after their attack and the subsequent mopping up.

Along the wall was a line of gray bundles and above them the stone was pitted with bullet holes. In a watchtower above the gate, a Chinese hugged his machine gun and the muzzle pointed at the afternoon sun. Small wisps of steam still rose from the burst water jacket.

Occasional troops of cavalry rode in from the plains, bringing fragments of the rear guard of the fleeing Chinese army. The prisoners were officers only, men who might wish to talk.

Above the entire area hung smoke, shredded and whipped away by the wind but ever rising like a shroud.

Mitchell stopped a hundred yards from the gate. Until now troops had been too busy with gray uniforms to bother about olive green. No PC had been established to the south as yet. But this high gate barred the way and the sentries were very stiff before it.

"James," quavered the reverend, "it is not too late to back away. If they know about us, it's prison! And your pass may include details! James—"

"Shut up," growled Toughey mechanically. "Leave the sarge alone!"

They had their breath back and Mitchell took up the stretcher again. The reverend did his dance with more steps than ever, his eyes fixed on the next stopping place—the gate.

Mitchell glanced at the low-hanging sun. It was crimson an hour above the rim of the world. He looked at the walls ahead and the soldiers there. The shadows of the men were incredibly long.

"March," said Mitchell.

They advanced slowly. Ahead of them the sentries stirred. An officer's red bands could be seen as he stopped a few paces forward to stare at the oncoming party.

Mitchell approached within ten feet and set down his burden. The reverend was staring so widely at the officer that he forgot to lower his end, leaving Toughey's head much lower than his feet.

With brisk military precision, Mitchell produced the pass and handed it over. The officer's small face brightened and he glanced up.

"United States, so?"

"United States Marines," said Mitchell. "I am under orders to report to the United States Consulate of this city."

But "United States, so?" was the entire fund of English at the officer's disposal. He shrugged and then fell to examining the pass again. Three of his guard had advanced within thrusting distance and the reverend changed his attention to the points of their bayonets, one of which was reddish black halfway to the hilt. He was still holding his end of the stretcher in the air and Toughey was too intent to protest.

"United States, so?" said the officer again, looking up.

"Yes," said Mitchell. "United States, *so*." And he pointed past the officer toward the gate.

The officer suddenly understood and once more examined the identity pass. Then, evidently thinking that Mitchell could be no less than a captain, he saluted and bowed.

Mitchell saluted and bowed, waiting to see what would happen.

The officer shouted, *"Mon o akero!"* and saluted and bowed again. Mitchell saluted and bowed and the big gate was slowly opened by the sentries. He put the pass back in his pocket and picked up the stretcher.

"March," said Mitchell.

They passed through the gate and into the littered street beyond.

"I told you he had brains," said Toughey. "We're in Shunkien!"

Ahead of them, whipping proudly against the sky, was the Stars and Stripes.

Chapter Sixteen

THE machinery salesman heard the knocking at the gate and he hurried into Jackson's office. "Somebody wants in, Jackson."

"It's the Japanese," said Jackson, running his fingers through his white hair. "A lot of good *they'll* do us."

He went through the packed corridors and the Americans watched him pass with dull eyes. The machinery salesman had talked and now that two men were down, their hope was gone.

Jackson heard the knock repeated as he carefully let down the bars of the small door, expecting to see an officer's red band.

Mitchell saluted with precision.

"Gunnery Sergeant Mitchell and party reporting to Consul Jackson, Shunkien."

Stunned, Jackson could only gape until Toughey raised up on his stretcher and said, "Well, what the hell are you waiting for? Christmas?"

"The Marines," whispered Jackson. "I thought . . . I thought . . ."

"I was ordered to be here by Saturday and it's Saturday," said Mitchell.

Jackson recovered himself and began to grin. He threw the door wide and marched off in front, spring coming back into his stride, chest expanding, white hair starting straight up from his head.

As they passed through the corridor, people stared in disbelief and then, as they went by leaped up and jammed the passage. A young oil scout whistled shrilly and the machinery salesman bellowed with joy. And then the cannonade of the week before was nothing compared to the din within the consulate.

The group reached Jackson's office and the reverend gladly deposited his end on the rug at Mitchell's command. But the noise outside was too great for any conversation. With difficulty, Jackson shut the jammed door.

The young radio operator grinned up at Mitchell.

"They've come, Billy!" cried Jackson as though Billy could not see for himself. "They've come! You've been hammering that key for days asking, pleading for them and now they're here!"

"Got a cigarette?" said Billy.

The doctor, whose eyes were further than ever back in his round skull, came from another room. Hurriedly he stepped up to Mitchell.

"Quick! Have you got that serum? I can save the lot if you have."

"Serum?" said Mitchell blankly. "Oh. This box. Was *that* what was in it?" He unstrapped it from his web belt and handed it over.

The doctor grabbed it like a hound grabs steak. He whisked himself out of the place and his voice could be heard outside getting the Americans in line.

Jackson saw Toughey then. "There's a bed in the next room. My bed. If you care to use it. . . ."

"Father," said Mitchell. "The stretcher."

The reverend struggled with it and got it off the floor and they carried Toughey away to a soft bunk.

The doctor had made this his sick bay and a few medical supplies were scattered on the table. Mitchell glanced at them as he eased Toughey's head to the pillow.

"Dress his wound," said Mitchell to the reverend. "Right away and do a good job on it."

The reverend looked resignedly at his son. And then he peeled off his coat and rolled up his sleeves and started to work.

"We made it," said Toughey.

"Did you think we wouldn't?"

"Well, for a while there I had my doubts, Sarge. What with you packin' a bottle . . ." He stopped too late and then saw that Mitchell was grinning at him. "Well, we made it anyhow. I always said you could go to hell and come back draggin' the devil by the tail."

The reverend looked shocked.

"Maybe I have," said Mitchell.

He was still grinning when he went out and closed the door.

Goldy was sitting in Jackson's chair. She looked up when Mitchell came in and followed him across the room with her eyes.

He stopped beside the operator. "Can you send a message to the USS *Miami* for me?"

"I know that call by heart, leatherneck. Here's paper."

"You take it," said Mitchell. "Commanding Officer, Marine

115

Detachment, USS *Miami*. Have reported to United States Consul Jackson, Shunkien, delivering box and keg. Mitchell, James, gunnery sergeant USMC."

The operator threw his starter switch and began to rattle his bug. Mitchell saw another door beyond him framing a white bed. He walked very briskly toward it, carrying himself in a military manner.

Goldy had seen men walk that way before, just before they fell flat on their faces. In some alarm she started up and kept Mitchell from closing the door on her.

She edged in, looking up at him watchfully. She eased the door closed behind her.

"Sit down on that bed," said Goldy.

Mitchell had about-faced in the middle of the room. He started to smile at her and then stopped. He was suddenly the color of whitewash.

"Don't care if I do," he said unsteadily, and half sat, half fell upon the covers.

Goldy squared him around. She unbuttoned his overcoat and braced him up while she took it off him. His blouse followed and she let him lie back. She was unloosening the khaki-colored tie and she saw his side.

"You're hit! Look!"

"I don't have to look," said Mitchell, his eyes closed.

"You were hit the same time Toughey was!" she accused in great alarm. "Oh, you fool. Why didn't . . . ?"

"We got here, didn't we?" whispered Mitchell.

She had unbuttoned his shirt and she saw that he had a crude bandage on his side.

"Does it . . . does it hurt much?" she said.

"It's just a scratch," whispered Mitchell. "Gimme a drink. The bottle's . . . bottle's in my pack."

She gave him a drink and he lay back, eyes still closed. She stared at him, frightened, her heart thundering in her throat. She turned, almost in a panic, and hurried toward the door.

"Stop," said Mitchell.

"But the doctor . . ."

"It's not that bad," said Mitchell, not moving or even winking. "I got kind of worn out the last couple miles. That's all. Just kind of worn out. Come back and sit down." He patted the cover with his hand and his eyes were still shut and his face was very white.

She stood where she was, still uncertain about getting the doctor.

"I won't make a pass at you," whispered Mitchell with a faint grin.

Everything was suddenly misty to her. She sat down gently on the edge of the bed.

"Now put the bottle on the table there," said Mitchell. "Put it so the label is facing me."

She obeyed.

"Got it?" said Mitchell. "Now wait a minute. I'm going to look at it. Maybe it will say 'Give strong drink unto him that is ready to perish, and wine unto those that be of heavy hearts. Proverbs 31:6.' And maybe it will just say 'Canadian Whisky. Five Years Old. One Quart.'"

He lifted himself slowly on his elbow and opened his eyes.

117

He stared for a long time at the bottle and then grinned a little as he lay back.

"It said 'Canadian Whisky. Five Years Old. One Quart.'" He chuckled about it and was silent for a long time. Then suddenly he opened his eyes and grinned at her. "Did you see him asleep in the car?"

Abruptly Goldy understood. "Do you want another drink?"

"No, thanks. Later maybe." He seemed to get stronger and his grin broadened. "Toughey says I could go down to hell and come back dragging the devil by his tail." He stopped and propped himself up on his elbow and took Goldy's hand. "I guess I could—now."

He looked better and she smiled at him. "Want that drink yet?"

"No," said Mitchell, laughing aloud. "Hell, no. I'm not ready to perish, am I?"

And back aboard the *Miami*, Captain Davis reported in a rush to the captain's quarters, so precipitately that he carried his dinner napkin with him and tried to salute, bare-headed, with the napkin in his right hand.

And then he saw Blackstone's unclouded visage and beheld the uncrumpled radiogram in the captain's big fingers. Blackstone was reading it over and over and Davis, seeing that it was addressed to himself, took the liberty of reading it over his shoulder.

Davis grinned and polished his palms on the napkin, subduing a desire to kiss the top of Blackstone's head.

Blackstone turned as though Davis had been there for hours.

"Great fellow, that Mitchell," said Blackstone. "I shall have to tell him so when he comes aboard. I guess I know how to run this ship, eh, Davis?"

"Yes, SIR!"

Story Preview

NOW that you've just ventured through one of the captivating tales in the Stories from the Golden Age collection by L. Ron Hubbard, turn the page and enjoy a preview of *Wind-Gone-Mad*. Join Jim Dahlgren, representative in China for the Amalgamated Aeronautical Company, who's had enough of the fatalistic brand of diplomacy that allows warlords like "The Butcher" to rise up in the provinces with weapons of fire and sword. But when Dahlgren disappears, supposedly to find a mysterious aviator called Feng-Feng to bring the Butcher's administration to its knees, he ignites a series of events which just may spell disaster.

Wind–Gone–Mad

THE square of yellow earth slid up over the motor cowl with appalling speed. The altimeter shot down to five hundred feet before the pilot whipped his ship into a slashing sideslip.

Men in gray uniforms were running away from deserted machine guns, disappearing behind piles of sandbags. An officer stopped to empty his automatic at the charging slash of color.

The pilot fishtailed wildly and shot over the stiff wind sock. The plane snapped suddenly into landing position. With a crunching slap, the ship was down.

It was as if an electric current had been shut off. Men began to fumble for their lost caps. Gunners slouched back to their pieces. The officer calmly slid another clip into his gun and holstered it. On the side of the red fuselage they had all seen the dragon and the two mammoth characters which identified their visitor. They knew this man and they also knew that he had little connection with The Butcher.

The pilot stood up in his narrow pit and stretched. But he did not remove the goggles which hid a quarter of his face, nor did he so much as unfasten the chin strap of the lurid helmet he wore.

The officer, a White Russian, stopped and looked at the red

dragon which spat fire above the pilot's eyes and then curled down around the ear pads. Assured of the man's identity, he came forward again.

"I am sorry, Feng-Feng. Had I but seen the dragon—"

"Quite all right," interrupted the pilot. "I wish an audience with Cheng-Wang immediately."

"Cheng-Wang is at your service, I am sure. But perhaps it would be better for us to place your plane in a bombproof hangar. We are waiting an attack by The Butcher. Perhaps if we service your engine, when the bombers come you can—"

Wind-Gone-Mad laughed joyously. "Such faith! You think that I would attack three Demming bombers single-handed? Really, my good friend Blakely sells better ships than you suppose. I would be downed in an instant."

It was the Russian's turn to laugh. Wind-Gone-Mad shot down? The thing was impossible, ludicrous. In a moment he subsided and spoke again more seriously. "Had Cheng-Wang listened better to the proposition to buy three Amalgamated bombers when you asked—"

"Quiet," said Feng-Feng, not unkindly. "That is a secret that only a few of us hold. Its release would mean my death. But never mind. I go to see Cheng-Wang. Service my ship and listen in on my panel radio for talk in Shen Province. The pigs will give you warning. If you know that they come, send for me and I will do my best to beat them off." He dropped to the ground lightly and strode toward a waiting motorcycle.

Cheng-Wang was old. On his parchment face was stamped the weariness of one who has seen too much, has fought too many battles, has witnessed too often the summer's fading into the dusty harshness of winter.

Cheng-Wang was frail and when he moved his hands the almost-fleshless bones clattered above the click of his long fingernails. With an impassive nod, he gave the order that the man called Feng-Feng be admitted to the audience room.

Still masked by his goggles and casqued by his helmet, Wind-Gone-Mad entered with long, determined strides. His leather flying coat rustled when he sat down in the indicated chair.

"It pleases me that you come," said Cheng-Wang in five-toned Mandarin Chinese. "Long have I wanted to give you my regrets for not accepting your offer and your warning. Now there is little we can do. The Butcher has begun his fight and it will be short. Along the eastern border, my troops lose miles of ground each day. They are harassed from the air. But you have come too late."

Behind the lenses of the great goggles, Feng-Feng's gray eyes held those of the provincial governor. "I do not think that I have. Our friend Blakely sold them no pursuit planes because they could procure no pilots. At the North China Airways field I now have a fighting ship—my own. It has two machine guns and it travels four miles a minute. With that I can help you."

"It is useless," mourned Cheng-Wang. "I will not allow you to throw your life to The Butcher. You do it out of sympathy alone and you use no regard for your own safety. The Butcher has placed a price on you, and that long ago. He would see your helmeted head dangling from a picket. Blakely, the man

125

you oddly call your friend, negotiated that these many months gone by."

"There are no bombers at my call in Shanghai," stated the man called Feng-Feng. "I can only do as fate and my hand dictate. Is it true that you are to receive an air attack today?"

Without explanation, knowing that it was not needed, Cheng-Wang presented a square of paper which bore black slashes. Deciphered, it said:

> The Hawks of The Butcher strike before dark. It is better to accept an honorable surrender from Cheng-Wang than for The Butcher to occupy a lifeless town.

The massive black doors swung back and a soldier in gray stood rigidly at attention in the opening. He saluted. "To the east, heaven-borne, are the Hawks of The Butcher." Dropping his hand he left-faced, waiting for Wind-Gone-Mad to precede him out of the palace.

The pilot turned, and his mouth was set. "Refuse to know terror, Cheng-Wang. This one goes to dull the claws of The Butcher." He tramped rapidly away and the black doors swung softly shut behind him.

To find out more about *Wind-Gone-Mad* and how you can obtain your copy, go to www.goldenagestories.com.

Glossary

STORIES FROM THE GOLDEN AGE *reflect the words and expressions used in the 1930s and 1940s, adding unique flavor and authenticity to the tales. While a character's speech may often reflect regional origins, it also can convey attitudes common in the day. So that readers can better grasp such cultural and historical terms, uncommon words or expressions of the era, the following glossary has been provided.*

adagio dancers: performers of a slow dance sequence of well-controlled graceful movements including lifting, balancing and turning, performed as a display of skill.

Adonis: an extremely handsome young man; originating from the name of a beautiful youth in Greek mythology.

altimeter: a gauge that measures altitude.

Atlantic Fleet: the part of the Navy responsible for operations in and around the Atlantic Ocean. Originally formed in 1906, it has been an integral part of the defense of the US for most of the twentieth century.

batteries: groups of large-caliber weapons used for combined action.

Big Town: nickname for New York City.

bobtail: to curtail or reduce, as in rank.

boot: a Marine or Navy recruit in basic training.

brigand: one who lives by plunder; a bandit.

Browning, 1917: a light machine gun weighing fifteen pounds. It looks like and can be fired like an ordinary rifle, either from the shoulder or the hip. It was invented by John M. Browning (1855–1926), an American firearms designer.

bug: a high-speed telegrapher's key that makes repeated dots or dashes automatically and saves motion of the operator's hand.

bulldog toes: high rounded toes on shoes with thick soles.

carbine: a short rifle used in the cavalry.

casqued: having a military headpiece or helmet on.

cat's: cat's pajamas; cat's meow; someone or something wonderful or remarkable.

Château-Thierry: a town of northern France on the Marne River, east-northeast of Paris. It was the site of the second Battle of the Marne (June 3–4, 1918), which ended the last major German offensive in World War I.

Chi: Chicago.

cholera: an infectious disease of the small intestine, typically contracted from infected water.

C-in-C: Commander in Chief.

Clydes: Clydesdale; one of a Scottish breed of strong, hardy draft horses, having a feathering of long hairs along the backs of the legs, so called because they were bred in the valley of the Clyde in Scotland.

cork off: go to bed; sleep.

corn willy: canned corned beef hash.

cowl: a removable metal covering for an engine, especially an aircraft engine.

dixie: a mess tin or oval pot often used in camp for cooking or boiling (as tea).

Doko e yuku!: (Japanese) Where are you going!

embrasures: (in fortification) openings, as a loophole through which missiles may be discharged.

emplacements: prepared positions for weapons or military equipment.

fan dancer: a woman dancer who performs solo, nude or nearly nude, using fans for covering.

Frisco: San Francisco.

gangway: a narrow, movable platform or ramp forming a bridge by which to board or leave a ship.

Genghis Khan: (1162?–1227) Mongol conqueror who founded the largest land empire in history and whose armies, known for their use of terror, conquered many territories and slaughtered the populations of entire cities.

G-men: government men; agents of the Federal Bureau of Investigation.

golden guinea: a British coin worth twenty-one shillings (a shilling is one-twentieth of a pound).

gunwale: the upper edge of the side of a boat. Originally a gunwale was a platform where guns were mounted, and was designed to accommodate the additional stresses imposed by the artillery being used.

Hell to Halifax: a variation of the phrase "from here to Halifax," meaning everywhere, in all places no matter how far from here. "Halifax" is a county in eastern Canada, on the Atlantic Ocean.

howitzers: cannons that have comparatively short barrels, used especially for firing shells at a high angle of elevation for a short range, as for reaching a target behind cover or in a trench.

Huangpu: a long river in China flowing through Shanghai. It is a major navigational route, lined with wharves, warehouses and industrial plants, and provides access to Shanghai for oceangoing vessels.

ideographs: written symbols that represent an idea or object directly, rather than by particular words or speech sounds, as Chinese or Japanese characters.

jack: money.

Kawasaki KDA-5: a fighter biplane built by Kawasaki, a Japanese aircraft manufacturer founded in 1918. The first prototype flew in 1932; 380 of these planes were built.

key: a hand-operated device used to transmit Morse code messages.

leatherneck: a member of the US Marine Corps. The phrase comes from the early days of the Marine Corps when enlisted men were given strips of leather to wear around their necks. The popular concept was that the leather protected the neck from a saber slash, though it was actually used to keep the Marines from slouching in uniform by forcing them to keep their heads up.

Legation: the official headquarters of a diplomatic minister.

lighters: large open flat-bottomed barges, used in loading and unloading ships offshore or in transporting goods for short distances in shallow waters.

mean: unimposing or shabby.

men-o'-war: armed ships of a national navy usually carrying between twenty and one hundred and twenty guns.

Mex: Mexican peso; in 1732 it was introduced as a trade coin with China and was so popular that China became one of its principal consumers. Mexico minted and exported pesos to China until 1949. It was issued as both coins and paper money.

Mikado: the emperor of Japan; a title no longer used.

Mon o akero!: (Japanese) Open the gate!

Native Quarter: also Native City; deep in the center of Peking, far from the ordinary people, was the Forbidden City, where the Emperor resided and carried out the affairs of state. It was spread out over a large area with audience halls, libraries and theaters, all reserved solely for the emperor. Surrounding this area was the Imperial City, with granaries, temples, residences for high officials and workshops of artisans who provided services and goods for the imperial household. Circling that was the Tartar City, occupied by the military men; and to the south was the Native City, where the Chinese resided. Each of these cities within cities had its own walls, which were clearly organized and defined the status of its residents.

Nic: Nicaragua; from 1927 until 1933 there was guerrilla warfare against the Nicaraguan government and the US Marines that were sent to defend US interests.

Nippon: the native Japanese name for Japan.

OD: (military) olive drab.

Old Glory: a common nickname for the flag of the US, bestowed by William Driver (1803–1886), an early nineteenth-century American sea captain. Given the flag as a gift, he hung it from his ship's mast and hailed it as "Old Glory" when he left harbor for a trip around the world (1831–1832) as commander of a whaling vessel. Old Glory served as the ship's official flag throughout the voyage.

PC: Post Command; military installation where the command personnel are located.

Peking: now Beijing, China.

pince-nez: a pair of glasses held on the face by a spring that grips the nose.

Portsmouth: US Naval and Marine prison located in Maine and occupied from 1908 until 1974.

powder, took a: made a speedy departure; ran away.

radio: a radio message; a radiogram.

redeye: cheap, strong whisky.

Rising Sun: Japan; the characters that make up Japan's name mean "the sun's origin," which is why Japan is sometimes identified as the "Land of the Rising Sun." It is also the military flag of Japan and was used as the ensign of the Imperial Japanese Navy and the war flag of the Imperial Japanese Army until the end of World War II.

Scheherazade: the female narrator of *The Arabian Nights,* who during one thousand and one adventurous nights saved her life by entertaining her husband, the king, with stories.

scuppered: ruined; wrecked.

scuppers are under: when a ship is too heavily loaded that its scuppers (openings in the side of a ship at deck level that allow water to run off) are under water. Used figuratively.

sea anchor: a device, such as a conical canvas bag, that is thrown overboard and dragged behind a ship to control its speed or heading.

Shanghai: city of eastern China at the mouth of the Yangtze River, and the largest city in the country. Shanghai was opened to foreign trade by treaty in 1842 and quickly prospered. France, Great Britain and the United States all held large concessions (rights to use land granted by a government) in the city until the early twentieth century.

Shantung: the dialect spoken in Shantung, a peninsula in east China extending into the Yellow Sea.

Shen Province: also known as *Shensi* or *Shaanxi;* north central province neighboring Shan Province.

shin the chains: leave the ship without permission.

sideslip: (of an aircraft when excessively banked) to slide sideways, toward the center of the curve described in turning.

slip cable: to leave a place; part company. From the nautical phrase "to slip cable" which means to let go of the anchor cable (let it slip off the ship) when a quick departure is needed and time cannot be spared to raise the anchor.

stanchion: an upright bar, post or frame forming a support or barrier.

swagger coat: a woman's pyramid-shaped coat with a full flared back and usually raglan sleeves (sleeves extending to the collar of a garment instead of ending at the shoulder), first popularized in the 1930s.

taii: (Japanese) a lieutenant.

tanglefoot: a strong drink, especially cheap whisky.

three sheets to the wind: in a disordered state caused by drinking; intoxicated. This expression is generally thought to refer to the sheet (a rope or chain) that holds one or both lower corners of a sail. If the sheet is allowed to go slack in the wind, the sail flaps about and the boat is tossed about much as a drunk staggers. Having three sheets loose would presumably make the situation all the worse.

Tientsin: seaport located southeast of Peking; China's third largest city and major transportation and trading center. Tientsin was a "Treaty Port," a generic term used to denote Chinese cities open to foreign residence and trade, usually the result of a treaty.

tin can: an improvised hand grenade, made by filling tin cans with bits of iron and a high explosive in which a fuse cord was inserted. The cord was lighted and the can with the sputtering fuse was thrown into the enemy lines.

toesmithing: among people of the theater, a term for *dancing.*

tonneau: the rear seating compartment of an automobile.

trick: a period or turn of duty.

under weigh: in motion; underway.

USMC: United States Marine Corps.

USN: United States Navy.

USS: United States Ship.

"white man's burden": from a poem written by Rudyard Kipling originally published in 1899 with regard to the US conquest of the Philippines and other former Spanish colonies. Subject to different interpretations, it was latched onto by imperialists to justify colonialism as a noble enterprise. Much of Kipling's other writings suggested that he genuinely believed in the benevolent role that the introduction of Western ideas could play in lifting non-Western peoples out of "poverty and ignorance."

White Russian: a Russian who fought against the Bolsheviks (Russian Communist Party) in the Russian Revolution, and fought against the Red Army during the Russian Civil War from 1918 to 1921.

whitewash: a white liquid that is a mixture of lime or powdered chalk and water, used for making walls or ceilings white.

L. Ron Hubbard
in the Golden Age
of Pulp Fiction

*In writing an adventure story
a writer has to know that he is adventuring
for a lot of people who cannot.
The writer has to take them here and there
about the globe and show them
excitement and love and realism.
As long as that writer is living the part of an
adventurer when he is hammering
the keys, he is succeeding with his story.*

*Adventuring is a state of mind.
If you adventure through life, you have a
good chance to be a success on paper.*

*Adventure doesn't mean globe-trotting,
exactly, and it doesn't mean great deeds.
Adventuring is like art.
You have to live it to make it real.*

— L. RON HUBBARD

L. Ron Hubbard
and American
Pulp Fiction

B ORN March 13, 1911, L. Ron Hubbard lived a life at
least as expansive as the stories with which he enthralled
a hundred million readers through a fifty-year career.

Originally hailing from Tilden, Nebraska, he spent his
formative years in a classically rugged Montana, replete with
the cowpunchers, lawmen and desperadoes who would later
people his Wild West adventures. And lest anyone imagine
those adventures were drawn from vicarious experience, he
was not only breaking broncs at a tender age, he was also
among the few whites ever admitted into Blackfoot society
as a bona fide blood brother. While if only to round out an
otherwise rough and tumble youth, his mother was that rarity
of her time—a thoroughly educated woman—who introduced
her son to the classics of Occidental literature even before
his seventh birthday.

But as any dedicated L. Ron Hubbard reader will attest, his
world extended far beyond Montana. In point of fact, and as the
son of a United States naval officer, by the age of eighteen he
had traveled over a quarter of a million miles. Included therein
were three Pacific crossings to a then still mysterious Asia, where
he ran with the likes of Her British Majesty's agent-in-place

L. Ron Hubbard, left, at Congressional Airport, Washington, DC, 1931, with members of George Washington University flying club.

for North China, and the last in the line of Royal Magicians from the court of Kublai Khan. For the record, L. Ron Hubbard was also among the first Westerners to gain admittance to forbidden Tibetan monasteries below Manchuria, and his photographs of China's Great Wall long graced American geography texts.

Upon his return to the United States and a hasty completion of his interrupted high school education, the young Ron Hubbard entered George Washington University. There, as fans of his aerial adventures may have heard, he earned his wings as a pioneering barnstormer at the dawn of American aviation. He also earned a place in free-flight record books for the longest sustained flight above Chicago. Moreover, as a roving reporter for *Sportsman Pilot* (featuring his first professionally penned articles), he further helped inspire a generation of pilots who would take America to world airpower.

Immediately beyond his sophomore year, Ron embarked on the first of his famed ethnological expeditions, initially to then untrammeled Caribbean shores (descriptions of which would later fill a whole series of West Indies mystery-thrillers). That the Puerto Rican interior would also figure into the future of Ron Hubbard stories was likewise no accident. For in addition to cultural studies of the island, a 1932–33

LRH expedition is rightly remembered as conducting the first complete mineralogical survey of a Puerto Rico under United States jurisdiction.

There was many another adventure along this vein: As a lifetime member of the famed Explorers Club, L. Ron Hubbard charted North Pacific waters with the first shipboard radio direction finder, and so pioneered a long-range navigation system universally employed until the late twentieth century. While not to put too fine an edge on it, he also held a rare Master Mariner's license to pilot any vessel, of any tonnage in any ocean.

Yet lest we stray too far afield, there is an LRH note at this juncture in his saga, and it reads in part:

"I started out writing for the pulps, writing the best I knew, writing for every mag on the stands, slanting as well as I could."

To which one might add: His earliest submissions date from the summer of 1934, and included tales drawn from true-to-life Asian adventures, with characters roughly modeled on British/American intelligence operatives he had known in Shanghai. His early Westerns were similarly peppered with details drawn from personal experience. Although therein lay a first hard lesson from the often cruel world of the pulps. His first Westerns were soundly rejected as lacking the authenticity of a Max Brand yarn

Capt. L. Ron Hubbard in Ketchikan, Alaska, 1940, on his Alaskan Radio Experimental Expedition, the first of three voyages conducted under the Explorers Club flag.

(a particularly frustrating comment given L. Ron Hubbard's Westerns came straight from his Montana homeland, while Max Brand was a mediocre New York poet named Frederick Schiller Faust, who turned out implausible six-shooter tales from the terrace of an Italian villa).

Nevertheless, and needless to say, L. Ron Hubbard persevered and soon earned a reputation as among the most publishable names in pulp fiction, with a ninety percent placement rate of first-draft manuscripts. He was also among the most prolific, averaging between seventy and a hundred thousand words a month. Hence the rumors that L. Ron Hubbard had redesigned a typewriter for faster keyboard action and pounded out manuscripts on a continuous roll of butcher paper to save the precious seconds it took to insert a single sheet of paper into manual typewriters of the day.

That all L. Ron Hubbard stories did not run beneath said byline is yet another aspect of pulp fiction lore. That is, as publishers periodically rejected manuscripts from top-drawer authors if only to avoid paying top dollar, L. Ron Hubbard and company just as frequently replied with submissions under various pseudonyms. In Ron's case, the

---

A MAN OF MANY NAMES

Between 1934 and 1950, L. Ron Hubbard authored more than fifteen million words of fiction in more than two hundred classic publications. To supply his fans and editors with stories across an array of genres and pulp titles, he adopted fifteen pseudonyms in addition to his already renowned L. Ron Hubbard byline.

Winchester Remington Colt
Lt. Jonathan Daly
Capt. Charles Gordon
Capt. L. Ron Hubbard
Bernard Hubbel
Michael Keith
Rene Lafayette
Legionnaire 148
Legionnaire 14830
Ken Martin
Scott Morgan
Lt. Scott Morgan
Kurt von Rachen
Barry Randolph
Capt. Humbert Reynolds

---

list included: Rene Lafayette, Captain Charles Gordon, Lt. Scott Morgan and the notorious Kurt von Rachen—supposedly on the lam for a murder rap, while hammering out two-fisted prose in Argentina. The point: While L. Ron Hubbard as Ken Martin spun stories of Southeast Asian intrigue, LRH as Barry Randolph authored tales of romance on the Western range—which, stretching between a dozen genres is how he came to stand among the two hundred elite authors providing close to a million tales through the glory days of American Pulp Fiction.

L. Ron Hubbard, circa 1930, at the outset of a literary career that would finally span half a century.

In evidence of exactly that, by 1936 L. Ron Hubbard was literally leading pulp fiction's elite as president of New York's American Fiction Guild. Members included a veritable pulp hall of fame: Lester "Doc Savage" Dent, Walter "The Shadow" Gibson, and the legendary Dashiell Hammett—to cite but a few.

Also in evidence of just where L. Ron Hubbard stood within his first two years on the American pulp circuit: By the spring of 1937, he was ensconced in Hollywood, adopting a Caribbean thriller for Columbia Pictures, remembered today as *The Secret of Treasure Island*. Comprising fifteen thirty-minute episodes, the L. Ron Hubbard screenplay led to the most profitable matinée serial in Hollywood history. In accord with Hollywood culture, he was thereafter continually called upon

The 1937 Secret of Treasure Island, *a fifteen-episode serial adapted for the screen by L. Ron Hubbard from his novel,* Murder at Pirate Castle.

to rewrite/doctor scripts—most famously for long-time friend and fellow adventurer Clark Gable.

In the interim—and herein lies another distinctive chapter of the L. Ron Hubbard story—he continually worked to open Pulp Kingdom gates to up-and-coming authors. Or, for that matter, anyone who wished to write. It was a fairly unconventional stance, as markets were already thin and competition razor sharp. But the fact remains, it was an L. Ron Hubbard hallmark that he vehemently lobbied on behalf of young authors—regularly supplying instructional articles to trade journals, guest-lecturing to short story classes at George Washington University and Harvard, and even founding his own creative writing competition. It was established in 1940, dubbed the Golden Pen, and guaranteed winners both New York representation and publication in *Argosy*.

But it was John W. Campbell Jr.'s *Astounding Science Fiction* that finally proved the most memorable LRH vehicle. While every fan of L. Ron Hubbard's galactic epics undoubtedly knows the story, it nonetheless bears repeating: By late 1938, the pulp publishing magnate of Street & Smith was determined to revamp *Astounding Science Fiction* for broader readership. In particular, senior editorial director F. Orlin Tremaine called for stories with a stronger *human element*. When acting editor John W. Campbell balked, preferring his spaceship-driven tales, Tremaine enlisted Hubbard. Hubbard, in turn, replied with the genre's first truly *character-driven* works, wherein heroes are pitted not against bug-eyed monsters but the mystery and majesty of deep space itself—and thus was launched the Golden Age of Science Fiction.

The names alone are enough to quicken the pulse of any science fiction aficionado, including LRH friend and protégé, Robert Heinlein, Isaac Asimov, A. E. van Vogt and Ray Bradbury. Moreover, when coupled with LRH stories of fantasy, we further come to what's rightly been described as the foundation of every modern tale of horror: L. Ron Hubbard's immortal *Fear*. It was rightly proclaimed by Stephen King as one of the very few works to genuinely warrant that overworked term "classic"—as in: *"This is a classic tale of creeping, surreal menace and horror. . . . This is one of the really, really good ones."*

L. Ron Hubbard, 1948, among fellow science fiction luminaries at the World Science Fiction Convention in Toronto.

To accommodate the greater body of L. Ron Hubbard fantasies, Street & Smith inaugurated *Unknown*—a classic pulp if there ever was one, and wherein readers were soon thrilling to the likes of *Typewriter in the Sky* and *Slaves of Sleep* of which Frederik Pohl would declare: *"There are bits and pieces from Ron's work that became part of the language in ways that very few other writers managed."*

And, indeed, at J. W. Campbell Jr.'s insistence, Ron was regularly drawing on themes from the Arabian Nights and so introducing readers to a world of genies, jinn, Aladdin and Sinbad—all of which, of course, continue to float through cultural mythology to this day.

At least as influential in terms of post-apocalypse stories was L. Ron Hubbard's 1940 *Final Blackout*. Generally acclaimed as the finest anti-war novel of the decade and among the ten best works of the genre ever authored—here, too, was a tale that would live on in ways few other writers imagined.

Portland, Oregon, 1943; L. Ron Hubbard, captain of the US Navy subchaser PC 815.

Hence, the later Robert Heinlein verdict: "Final Blackout *is as perfect a piece of science fiction as has ever been written.*"

Like many another who both lived and wrote American pulp adventure, the war proved a tragic end to Ron's sojourn in the pulps. He served with distinction in four theaters and was highly decorated for commanding corvettes in the North Pacific. He was also grievously wounded in combat, lost many a close friend and colleague and thus resolved to say farewell to pulp fiction and devote himself to what it had supported these many years—namely, his serious research.

But in no way was the LRH literary saga at an end, for as he wrote some thirty years later, in 1980:

"Recently there came a period when I had little to do. This was novel in a life so crammed with busy years, and I decided to amuse myself by writing a novel that was pure *science fiction."*

That work was *Battlefield Earth: A Saga of the Year 3000.* It was an immediate *New York Times* bestseller and, in fact, the first international science fiction blockbuster in decades. It was not, however, L. Ron Hubbard's magnum opus, as that distinction is generally reserved for his next and final work: The 1.2 million word *Mission Earth.*

> **Final Blackout**
> *is as perfect
> a piece of
> science fiction
> as has ever
> been written.*
>
> —Robert Heinlein

How he managed those 1.2 million words in just over twelve months is yet another piece of the L. Ron Hubbard legend. But the fact remains, he did indeed author a ten-volume *dekalogy* that lives in publishing history for the fact that each and every volume of the series was also a *New York Times* bestseller.

Moreover, as subsequent generations discovered L. Ron Hubbard through republished works and novelizations of his screenplays, the mere fact of his name on a cover signaled an international bestseller. . . . Until, to date, sales of his works exceed hundreds of millions, and he otherwise remains among the most enduring and widely read authors in literary history. Although as a final word on the tales of L. Ron Hubbard, perhaps it's enough to simply reiterate what editors told readers in the glory days of American Pulp Fiction:

He writes the way he does, brothers, because he's been there, seen it and done it!

THE STORIES FROM THE GOLDEN AGE

Your ticket to adventure starts here with the Stories from
the Golden Age collection by master storyteller L. Ron Hubbard.
These gripping tales are set in a kaleidoscope of exotic locales and brim
with fascinating characters, including some of the
most vile villains, dangerous dames and brazen heroes
you'll ever get to meet.

The entire collection of over one hundred and fifty stories is being
released in a series of eighty books and audiobooks.
For an up-to-date listing of available titles,
go to www.goldenagestories.com.

AIR ADVENTURE

Arctic Wings	*Man-Killers of the Air*
The Battling Pilot	*On Blazing Wings*
Boomerang Bomber	*Red Death Over China*
The Crate Killer	*Sabotage in the Sky*
The Dive Bomber	*Sky Birds Dare!*
Forbidden Gold	*The Sky-Crasher*
Hurtling Wings	*Trouble on His Wings*
The Lieutenant Takes the Sky	*Wings Over Ethiopia*

FAR-FLUNG ADVENTURE

The Adventure of "X"
All Frontiers Are Jealous
The Barbarians
The Black Sultan
Black Towers to Danger
The Bold Dare All
Buckley Plays a Hunch
The Cossack
Destiny's Drum
Escape for Three
Fifty-Fifty O'Brien
The Headhunters
Hell's Legionnaire
He Walked to War
Hostage to Death

Hurricane
The Iron Duke
Machine Gun 21,000
Medals for Mahoney
Price of a Hat
Red Sand
The Sky Devil
The Small Boss of Nunaloha
The Squad That Never Came Back
Starch and Stripes
Tomb of the Ten Thousand Dead
Trick Soldier
While Bugles Blow!
Yukon Madness

SEA ADVENTURE

Cargo of Coffins
The Drowned City
False Cargo
Grounded
Loot of the Shanung
Mister Tidwell, Gunner

The Phantom Patrol
Sea Fangs
Submarine
Twenty Fathoms Down
Under the Black Ensign

TALES FROM THE ORIENT

The Devil—With Wings   *Pearl Pirate*
The Falcon Killer   *The Red Dragon*
Five Mex for a Million   *Spy Killer*
Golden Hell   *Tah*
The Green God   *The Trail of the Red Diamonds*
Hurricane's Roar   *Wind-Gone-Mad*
Inky Odds   *Yellow Loot*
Orders Is Orders

MYSTERY

The Blow Torch Murder   *The Grease Spot*
Brass Keys to Murder   *Killer Ape*
Calling Squad Cars!   *Killer's Law*
The Carnival of Death   *The Mad Dog Murder*
The Chee-Chalker   *Mouthpiece*
Dead Men Kill   *Murder Afloat*
The Death Flyer   *The Slickers*
Flame City   *They Killed Him Dead*

FANTASY

SCIENCE FICTION

WESTERN

The Baron of Coyote River   Man for Breakfast
Blood on His Spurs   The No-Gun Gunhawk
Boss of the Lazy B   The No-Gun Man
Branded Outlaw   The Ranch That No One Would Buy
Cattle King for a Day   Reign of the Gila Monster
Come and Get It   Ride 'Em, Cowboy
Death Waits at Sundown   Ruin at Rio Piedras
Devil's Manhunt   Shadows from Boot Hill
The Ghost Town Gun-Ghost   Silent Pards
Gun Boss of Tumbleweed   Six-Gun Caballero
Gunman!   Stacked Bullets
Gunman's Tally   Stranger in Town
The Gunner from Gehenna   Tinhorn's Daughter
Hoss Tamer   The Toughest Ranger
Johnny, the Town Tamer   Under the Diehard Brand
King of the Gunmen   Vengeance Is Mine!
The Magic Quirt   When Gilhooly Was in Flower

153

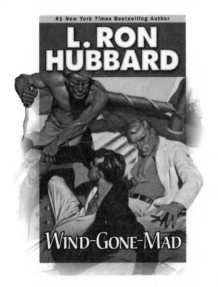

JOIN THE PULP REVIVAL
America in the 1930s and 40s

Pulp fiction was in its heyday and 30 million readers were regularly riveted by the larger-than-life tales of master storyteller L. Ron Hubbard. For this was pulp fiction's golden age, when the writing was raw and every page packed a walloping punch.

That magic can now be yours. An evocative world of nefarious villains, exotic intrigues, courageous heroes and heroines—a world that today's cinema has barely tapped for tales of adventure and swashbucklers.

Enroll today in the Stories from the Golden Age Club and begin receiving your monthly feature edition selected from more than 150 stories in the collection.

You may choose to enjoy them as either a paperback or audiobook for the special membership price of $9.95 each month along with FREE shipping and handling.

CALL TOLL-FREE: **1-877-8GALAXY**
(1-877-842-5299) OR GO ONLINE TO
www.goldenagestories.com
AND BECOME PART OF THE PULP REVIVAL!